OUR KIND OF LOVE

KAIT NOLAN

A LETTER TO READERS

Dear Reader,

This book is set in the Deep South. As such, it contains a great deal of colorful, colloquial, and occasionally grammatically incorrect language. This is a deliberate choice on my part as an author to most accurately represent the region where I have lived my entire life. This book also contains swearing and pre-marital sex between the lead couple, as those things are part of the realistic lives of characters of this generation, and of many of my readers.

If any of these things are not your cup of tea, please consider that you may not be the right audience for this book. There are scores of other books out there that are written with you in mind. In fact, I've got a list of some of my favorite authors who write on the sweeter side on my website at https://kaitnolan.com/on-the-sweeter-side/

If you choose to stick with me, I hope you enjoy!

Happy reading!

Kait

CHAPTER 1

Kyle Keenan was an ungrateful bastard. He didn't care about the arena of screaming fans begging for another encore, as he took his last bow of the night and faked a smile and affection for his tourmate, Mercy Lee Bradshaw. He didn't care that this tour had shot his current album up the charts. He didn't care that he was becoming a household name or that the True Country Network was calling him one of country music's shooting stars and had given him the award to prove it.

In this moment, all he gave a damn about was that this was the last stop on the tour. One more TV interview, then he was free. Free to go home. Free to rest and to breathe. Free to be a normal guy for a while and visit his little brother Caleb and his new wife. Free to closet himself in the studio to produce the next album. Not that he'd written a note of it yet.

The realities of life on tour had scared away the inspiration that used to tear through him with the bold, brash wildness of an untamed stallion. He'd need to coax it back like some shy forest creature, with time and patience—commodities that had been in increasingly dwindling supply over the past couple years. The music would come when his world wasn't full of so much other noise. And when it did, he'd find the love of it that had sent him out on the road at eighteen, determined to make something of himself. He just needed to get the hell off this stage and through the gauntlet to his tour bus.

As soon as the lights dimmed, he dropped Mercy Lee's hand, already jogging offstage and into the labyrinth of halls the public never saw.

A familiar, hulking shape separated itself from the shadows and fell into step beside him. "You look like you're ready to spit nails."

Griffin Powell never minced words. It was a trait Kyle had always appreciated about his foster brother. The shorthand they'd developed years ago was the sort that only arose between people who'd chosen to be family. That was what all the kids who'd gone through Joan Reynolds' home had become, regardless of how they'd ended up there. And thank God for it.

Vibrating with a restless, reckless energy, Kyle didn't spare him a glance. "I need to get out of here. My give a damn busted about five cities ago."

"On it." Griff shifted into what Kyle thought of as Tank Mode, clearing the path with nothing more than the breadth of his muscular shoulders and a back-the-hell-off attitude. That skill alone made hiring him for these last few months of the tour well worth it.

Because they expected it and because he understood the need to protect his image, Kyle dug deep to find a shred of the Nice Guy he tried so hard to be for the crew members and event staff who called out "Good show!" and "Congrats, man!" as he strode past. He mustered a semblance of a smile, accepting the back slaps and the fist bumps, but he let nothing deter him from his goal. He didn't even detour to his dressing room. The crew would finish packing his stuff, and he had a change of clothes on the bus.

His manager, Davis Lipscomb, appeared at his side. "You need to talk to the press."

"Nope. I talked to them before I performed. I already signed autographs and did my fan service. It's the last night, and I'm done with this dog and pony show." He'd spent the past six-plus months doing everything asked of him in the name of keeping his label happy. And that was fine. His memories of the lean years, when he'd played any gig that materialized and had lived out of his ancient Tahoe, grabbing showers at truck stops because he couldn't scrape together enough for a hotel, were still fresh enough in his mind that he was beyond grateful to *have* a label to please. But enough was enough.

Davis's mouth pressed into a thin line that telegraphed his displeasure. Kyle didn't give a shit about that, either. "You've still got the interview with *The Breakfast Club* tomorrow morning."

"I am aware. Why the hell do you think I'm so eager to get to the bus? I'd like at least a few hours of shuteye before I get back to Nashville." That was only part of the reason. He was so over every-damn-body wanting something from him, and he'd reached a level of fame where, once in a while, he could put himself first without fear he'd get dropped. With the numbers being reported for this latest album, the label damned well better recognize he deserved a vacation. God knew he needed one.

Dialing up his trademark Nice Guy smile one more time for the night, Kyle shoved out the back door, preceded by Griff, and flanked by a couple of guys from venue security. The crowd was already three- and four-deep along the roped-off path leading to the buses. How the hell did they get around here so fast? As always, his first instinct was to flinch at the attention and find somewhere to hide. But these were fans, not press, and he'd come a long way from that teenaged boy.

Determined, Kyle made his way down the line, nodding and waving, aware of the cameras and video he never escaped. His gaze passed right over the woman at first. But it came back for a fraction of a second, tugged by something in her eyes. The same bold blue as his own, though age and experience had hardened them.

The punch of shock made his steps falter.

It was enough.

She called his name. Not the one he'd adopted when he'd left his past behind, but the one he'd been given at birth. The sound of it should've gotten lost. Everyone around him was chanting his chosen name and cheering. But he heard the rasp of her voice—familiar, despite the distance of years. The sound of it pulled him back to that teenage boy again. To the stand he'd made that changed everything.

How had he not known she was out of prison?

Griff's hand nudged him forward. "Keep moving."

The touch grounded Kyle. He didn't acknowledge her, just fell back into motion with his brother. Was she alone? He didn't dare look, didn't dare react and risk giving the public or whatever paparazzi lurked among them something to latch onto. They were always circling, like carrion birds, in search of the next salacious meal of gossip. He'd worked way too damned hard and long at keeping this part of his past under wraps to slip up now.

At the door of his tour bus, he paused, sensing Davis at his shoulder. "Did you see her?"

"Yeah."

"Take care of it."

Without waiting for confirmation from his manager, he stepped onto the bus behind Griff, not quite breathing until the driver shut the door.

Pete beamed at him. "Last night, Mr. Keenan."

"Thank God."

The driver laughed. "Ready to get home?"

"You know it."

"We'll probably be another forty-five min-utes to an hour before getting on the road."

Kyle offered a more genuine smile to the older man, who'd seen that he and his band got from place to place for the last several months. "Not a problem. I'm gonna head on back, try to catch some Z's."

Pete saluted.

The drawn blinds gave an illusion of privacy from the hordes. Resisting the urge to lift them and press his face to the glass to scan the crowd for another glimpse of that face, Kyle passed his brother and strode to the back, grateful he'd graduated to a bus where he got an actual full-size bed instead of the narrow bunks that lined the hall, three-high on each side, where his backup band—and now Griff —slept when they were on the road. The sliding door gave him a little more of that illusory privacy, enough that he let the mask drop, let his hands shake. Without a word, Griff opened a cabinet in the wall and pulled out the bottle of rye whiskey, pouring a generous glass and handing it over.

Ghosts certainly called for it.

Kyle tossed back a healthy swallow, waiting as the alcohol burned through the initial shock, leaving him a little steadier. "What the actual hell is she doing here?"

Griff's military training showed as he

ranged himself in front of the door. "Don't know. Could make a few educated guesses. You aren't gonna like any of them."

Kyle pinched the bridge of his nose and sank into the chair. "Hasn't she fucked up my life enough? Haven't they both?"

"Reckon they feel the same way about you." At his sharp look, Griff lifted his hands for peace. "I'm just sayin'. It's not surprising she sought you out."

Maybe this was just another sign that he couldn't escape from his past. Their mistakes weren't his, but that hadn't stopped him from trying to atone for them. He'd made plenty of his own along the way. Reaching into his pocket, he fished out the talisman he kept to remind him of that fact.

The plastic ring was faded with age, the faux diamond scratched and the gold paint of the band flaked off in places from years riding in his pocket with loose change and a Swiss Army knife he'd carried even longer. Griff said nothing as Kyle ran his finger over the band, grounded by the slightly rough edges of plastic where it hadn't been properly trimmed from the mold. A long, long time ago, he'd given this ring and his heart to his best friend in the world, the woman he'd known he wanted to marry, even at the tender age of six. Twenty-five years of life experience hadn't changed his mind, but he'd unforgivably screwed that up. Abbey had sent the ring back, and he'd kept it ever since as a reminder that there were more important things than fame. He might not be able to make up for his mistakes with her, but he spent his time not on the road or in the studio working on balancing the karmic scales for the rest of his past.

The door slid open, and Kyle closed his fist around the ring.

Griff stepped aside so Davis could enter.

"The... situation... has been handled."

Kyle didn't want the details about how. "Just tell me one thing. Is he out?"

No need to specify who. Davis was the one

who'd helped bury the connection all these years. "He is not."

"Alright then." He drained the last of his glass. "I'm going to bed."

"Fine. But before we get to Nashville for tomorrow's interview, I wanted to talk to you."

Griff's gaze flicked toward Davis and back in silent question. Grateful beyond measure that someone he trusted had his back, Kyle nodded. He could handle his manager. With a faint jerk of his head in acknowledgment, Griff slipped out the door, leaving them alone.

"Alright. Talk fast. I'm tired."

"You should reconsider a relationship with Mercy Lee. She's country music's greatest darling right now. Being linked to her beyond the tour would really raise your profile, and tomorrow's a great opportunity to do that."

Kyle scowled and cut him off. "The answer is no. I'm not interested in fake or real dating that woman for any amount of exposure. We talked about this after that publicity stunt last fall." The lip-lock she'd sprung on him had been in the tabloids for months.

"Have I ever steered you wrong?"

The ring in his hand felt hot. But that was old ground and not something Kyle wanted to get into tonight. He uncoiled from his chair and advanced on the manager who'd been pushing and shoving him in directions he hadn't wanted for a while now. It stopped tonight. "What you're suggesting isn't a career move. It's my life. So, no. Final answer, and I won't discuss this again."

Something flashed in Davis' eyes—more disapproval, probably—but he didn't challenge Kyle again. "Get some sleep and try to remember the hosts are expecting country music's Captain America tomorrow."

That silly moniker they'd saddled him with because of his all-American good looks and Nice Guy charm. If only they knew where he came from.

"I'm aware of my role here." He'd been playing it for a lot of years now.

Davis flashed the genial shark's grin that he took into contract negotiations. "See you in the morning."

As soon as he stepped into the hall, Kyle shut and locked the sliding door and wondered when he'd stopped trusting the man whose job was to look out for his best interests.

He opened his fist and stared at the ring again for a long moment. Then, instead of falling into bed as he'd intended, he reached for his guitar.

AT THE CRASH of shattering glass, Abbey bolted through the backdoor, into the kitchen, to find her grandfather scowling and her mother clenching a dishtowel in white-knuckled fingers.

"Honestly, Roy."

"I don't *want* turnip greens!"

Abbey eyed the food among the shards of

plate on the floor. It appeared to be a spinach salad. That kind of day, then. She slid past the mess to a grab the dustpan and whisk broom from under the sink. "Take a break. I've got it."

Faye turned away and braced her hands on the counter, her silvering blonde hair falling forward to hide her face and the inevitable tears. They'd all shed plenty since their journey with his dementia began.

Abbey worked up a cheerful smile and crouched to sweep up the mess. "Hey, Granddaddy."

"Hey, Butter Bean! How was school today? Did you pass that algebra test?"

Though she was more than a decade past high-school graduation, Abbey rolled with the conversation. "Aced it, as always." When he was caught in the past, it was just easier to indulge him than to try to bring him back to now.

He slapped his knee. "That's my girl!"

"How was your day?"

"Up to my elbows in the engine of the

truck. Damned thing's making that knocking noise again."

She hoped he hadn't been trying to "fix" the engine on his own. They already had to hide the keys to keep him from trying to drive anything. With another glance at her mother, she dumped the mess into the trash and shifted into redirect mode.

"Want to split an apple and peanut butter before dinner?" She lowered her voice to a conspiratorial whisper. "We won't tell Mom." If he was in a recalcitrant eating mood, she could always coax him into eating an apple, so at least he had something nutritious.

Granddaddy tapped the side of his nose and grinned to acknowledge the shared secret. The man loved the idea of getting away with stuff.

Grabbing one of the glossy red Rome Beauties from a bowl on the counter and the jar of peanut butter from the pantry, she dropped into a chair beside her favorite person in the world and told him about her fictional day, filling it with things she remembered from high school. Not too hard since she'd gone to school with most of the folks she now worked with at the Misfit Spa, just outside Eden's Ridge. After a few minutes, her mom returned to dinner prep. Engaged with the everyday stories, Granddaddy ate the apple slices, not noticing that she gave him all of them. By the time she neared the end of the apple, her dad came in.

"Whatever's for dinner smells amazing, hon." Mark kissed the lines of strain on her mother's brow.

"Sure does," Granddaddy agreed. "Kyle better hurry on up, or he'll be late."

Abbey's hands fisted in her lap, as they always did when Granddaddy brought up Kyle like he was still a daily part of their lives, still part of the family. "He's not here for dinner tonight."

"Oh, too bad. I was hoping to get him to play for us after dinner."

The memory of all the nights he'd done exactly that had Abbey's throat going tight. It had been ten years. Would the mere mention of him ever stop being a knife through the heart?

This time, it was her father who stepped in to do the rescuing. "Actually, Dad, I was hoping to talk to you about some plans for the north orchard."

As Faye served dinner, talk turned to the business of apples—the thing most of her family had devoted their lives to for four generations. The conversation didn't take much participation on her part. Abbey found her mind wandering to Kyle. It didn't matter that she'd cut him out of her life a decade ago. Didn't matter that he hadn't been home in longer than that. He was so much a part of her history here that his echo was everywhere.

No matter how much she wanted to forget him, there was no living back in Eden's Ridge without having reminders, even without Granddaddy's memory lapses. She worked with his foster sisters, hung out right next door to where he'd spent his high school years, and saw the house where he'd grown up, a stone's throw from her own, every time she stepped outside.

At least she'd been living in Atlanta when everything had blown all to hell. She'd been able to hide her devastation. As far as anyone else knew, they'd had some kind of falling out and drifted apart. She'd never breathed a word of the truth about what had happened. Better she be the only one he hurt. But God, she wished she could make him as unimportant to her as she was to him. Wished, too, that she could stop him from starring in her fantasies. But Dream Abbey was as much of a fool as ever.

Talk shifted from the orchard to town gossip, providing a decent distraction from her thoughts.

"I heard they broke ground on the new small business incubator this week," Mark said.

Relieved to have something to contribute

to the conversation, Abbey jumped in. "Oh, yeah, Maggie said things are moving right along with that. They're hoping to open the doors later this fall."

"I don't know how she's going to juggle that *and* the Artisan Guild *and* a baby," Faye remarked.

"I'm pretty sure she's looking for someone else to take over management of the Guild."

They continued to discuss potential candidates for that. By the end of the meal, Granddaddy was back in the now, and he'd eaten the spinach salad without complaint.

"Well, I reckon I'll turn in. Got an early day tomorrow. Faye, that was delicious. Thank you." Granddaddy shoved back from the table, and they all braced to see how his balance would be. He took a staggering step or two before leveling out.

"I'll walk up with you. I need to grab some stuff for the laundry." Mark trailed him out of the room, ready and waiting to make sure Granddaddy navigated the stairs okay.

Faye began to rise, but Abbey pressed her back into her chair. "I've got the dishes, Mom. You take a few."

Her mother scrubbed both hands over her face, no longer trying to hide the exhaustion. "He was agitated all day until you got home."

"You know it's because I look like Grandma Ruth. And because I'm his favorite."

"You are that."

Abbey scraped, rinsed, and loaded plates into the dishwasher and started in on the pots and pans. She finished up with the last one as her dad came back into the room.

"He's settled." Mark sank into a chair himself and took his wife's hand.

Draping the dishtowel over the ledge of the sink, Abbey inhaled a bracing breath and turned to face her parents. "I have something I want to talk to you both about."

Faye paled even more. "What?"

Abbey *hated* that her mother's first thought was that it was something bad. "The last couple of years have been really draining. You both need a break. A real one. More than the occasional treatment at the spa." Crossing the room, she pulled the packet out of her purse. "So, you're going to take one."

Her dad frowned. "What are you talking about, baby?"

Extracting the contents of the manilla folder, she slid the slick brochure across the kitchen table. "I've arranged for you to take a ten-day cruise to the Caribbean."

"Don't be crazy. We can't up and go off on vacation. Your grandfather—"

"Does well with me. It's the off-season for the orchard, and Lewis and Ryder have things well-in-hand if anything comes up. It's your thirty-fifth anniversary. I've already bought the tickets and everything. You leave out of Mobile tomorrow afternoon."

Tears glittered in Faye's eyes. "You shouldn't have done this, honey. We can't go."

"Yes, you can. I've already made arrangements with all my friends to help, and I talked to Farrah Murchison about putting him in programming at the senior center to try it out. We've got everything here covered. You already hadn't been on a vacation in more years than I can count before his dementia hit. Let me do this for you."

Mark was looking a little watery himself. "I… don't know what to say."

"Say you'll go and have a good time and know I've got everything covered back here. Granddaddy and I will be fine." She might need a vacation herself when it was through, but it would be worth it to give her parents this gift.

Her mother opened the brochure. "There's all-you-can-eat buffets and onboard music. And snorkeling! I always wanted to try snorkeling."

Mark wrapped an arm around her shoulders and squeezed, and Abbey knew she had them. "Okay then, we'll go snorkeling." He reached out his free hand to take Abbey's. "Thank you for this. It already means so much that you moved home to help with Dad. This is above and beyond."

"It's what you deserve." Shoving back from the table, she made a shooing motion. "Now, hurry on up. Y'all need to pack."

CHAPTER 2

*S*craps of melody danced around the edges of Kyle's brain, as he waited in the green room to go on *The Breakfast Club*, Nashville's hottest, syndicated morning show. He itched to discharge this last duty so he could go back to his loft and write. This was the first glimmer of something new he'd had in longer than he cared to admit. If he had to reschedule his dinner plans with Caleb and Emerson to chase it, they'd understand.

He'd stayed up way too late, losing out on hours of precious sleep, coaxing out the lyrics.

Like all his biggest hits, the song was a heart-breaker, which meant it was the truest thing he'd written in a long time. Maybe it was time to stop hiding the pain and bleed it out into music. It said a lot that he found *that* more appealing than contemplating what it meant that his mother had shown up last night.

He rolled the ring across his knuckles like a coin. Would Abbey listen if he poured the whole thing out in a song? Give him the chance to explain, at last? Or had she cut his music as thoroughly out of her life as she had him?

A woman in a headset walked in. "You're up, Mr. Keenan."

He rose, pocketing the ring, and followed her to the sound stage in time to catch the tail end of the host's introduction. "—the most recent recipient of TCN's Shooting Star Award, and arguably one of the nicest guys in country music, please welcome Kyle Keenan!"

Smile in place, hand lifted to the cameras, he strode on stage to join the host, Jillian Jessop. He gave the expected air kiss on her cheek and dropped into the waiting chair, forcing himself to sit back and relax rather than perching on the edge of the seat.

"Thanks for joining us this morning."

"Thanks for having me." Kyle tried not to squint in the glare of the studio lights. It was too damned early for lights this bright. They beat down on him and sweat beaded between his shoulders. Or maybe that was the anxiety. He'd performed in front of hundreds of thousands of people without blinking, but that was with a guitar in his hands. He felt naked and exposed without one.

"Now, you just finished up the *Light My Fire* tour with Mercy Lee Bradshaw."

"Yes, ma'am. Just last night at the FedEx Forum in Memphis. After all these months on the road, it's good to be back in Tennessee."

"What's the plan for your down time?"

"Hanging out with my family and working on songs for the next album."

"Ooo, any hints about the direction that's taking?"

Instead of rubbing his sweaty palms on his jeans, he winked. "It's a surprise." *Even to me.*

Jillian pursed her lips. "Okay, okay. Let's talk about your most recent album, *Bustin' at the Seams*. It's currently number nine on the Billboard charts. What's it like breaking into that top ten?"

"I mean, it's amazing. That's been one of the things on my bucket list. It's incredibly humbling to have that many people enjoying my music, and I absolutely couldn't do it without them. Fans are everything."

"On that album is your first number one hit, "Hollow". Can we talk you into playing for us?"

The studio audience cheered. Relieved to have something to do besides just talk, Kyle nodded and accepted the guitar a stagehand brought out. He made a few adjustments to the tuning by ear. It had been ages since he'd done a solo acoustic version of this. Not since he'd cut the track in the studio. As he closed his eyes and began to play, the audience faded and he lost himself in the song, the story. Something about stripping away all the frills, all the polish, made the song more raw and took him back to when he'd written it. It was a song about grief and regret, everything he'd drowned in for the weeks and months after he'd realized Abbey was through with him. There was something karmic about this being his first number one, ensuring he relived all of it over and over, never letting the wound scab over.

The applause brought him back. Jillian clutched a few notecards to her chest, looking half ready to swoon. "I absolutely see why that's become the latest anthem for the broken-hearted. So easy for people to relate to."

Kyle kept the guitar in his lap, needing something in his hands to stop himself from reaching for the ring. "I think that's something the best songs have in common. They're the ones that connect to the human experience. Everybody's lost somebody."

Jillian's gaze turned shrewd. "Now, you yourself have been notoriously single since you entered the public eye. But you and Mercy Lee looked pretty cozy on the tour. Are your days of singlehood and sad songs coming to an end?"

His fingers clenched on the guitar as he struggled to hold on to his temper. He'd said in advance that this topic was off limits. A quick glance to the side showed Davis flashing an I-know-best smile. This shit needed to stop.

"Rumors of our involvement have been greatly exaggerated. Mercy Lee and I are just friends." They weren't even that, but it wasn't good for his image to air his true opinion of the woman on live national television.

"Come now, there's no reason to play your cards so close to your vest," Jillian cajoled.

"The fact is, I can't be involved with Mercy Lee because I'm already promised to someone else." And it didn't much matter to his heart that she'd sent back the ring. He didn't want anyone else.

The host gaped. "You heard it here first, ladies and gentlemen. Kyle Keenan is *engaged!*"

"Wait—" That wasn't what he'd meant, wasn't what he'd *said.* Was it?

But Jillian was like a shark scenting blood. "Tell us everything. Who is she? How long have y'all been together? How did you meet?"

Kyle scrambled to salvage the situation. Maybe he could make it clear he was off the market without this blowing up in his face. "She's the only one who's ever mattered. We've known each other forever, but she values her privacy, so we've kept everything on the down low. That won't be changing."

"That's all you're going to give us? Not even the story of your romance?"

Again with the Nice Guy smile. "That's it." Let the media chase their tails trying to figure out who he was talking about. There wasn't enough here for them to connect it to an actual person. It would be okay.

"Fine. I suppose we'll have to accept that. Let's wrap up with a lightning round of questions."

Dodged that bullet. Kyle relaxed. "Alright, let's do it."

"Favorite food?"

"Apple pie."

"Song you sing in the shower?"

"'The Thunder Rolls.'"

"Dogs or cats?"

"Dogs."

"Last book you read?"

"Blake Iverson's latest."

"Your girl's name."

"Abbey."

"Ah *ha!*"

Oh shit, what have I done? "That was dirty."

Jillian just shrugged, unrepentant. "Inquiring minds wanted to know. Thanks for joining us today." She turned her gaze back to the camera. "After the break, we'll be back with—"

But Kyle heard nothing else. He was too busy holding in the *oh shit, oh shit, oh shit* echoing through his skull like a refrain. He'd said her name. Not her last name. But if anybody did any real digging, tracing him back to Eden's Ridge, they'd find her. She'd be mobbed with media, and they wouldn't care what the truth was… Whether they were together or not, she'd be the center of a shitstorm.

This was all Davis's fault. If he hadn't pressed the Mercy Lee thing, Kyle's mouth wouldn't have run away without his brain. As soon as he got the all clear, he strode off the stage, yanking off his mic pack and shoving it at a nearby tech. His manager looked apoplectic.

Before he could even say a word, Kyle was in his face. "You're fired."

For a moment, legitimate shock blanked out the anger. "You don't mean that."

"Oh, I sure as hell do. We're done." There was satisfaction in saying it. In meaning it.

"About damned time," Griff muttered.

Color swept the other man's cheeks. "You'll regret this. You'd be nothing without me."

Perhaps that had been true once, but not anymore.

"I'll take my chances. Don't forget about the NDA you signed." Without a backward glance, he left Davis in the wings and headed for the studio exit, his brother right behind.

"Gonna be fallout from that," Griff observed.

"It'll be nothing compared to the hell that'll be unleashed if I don't get to Abbey before she hears about this interview." In truth, she was probably gonna kill him either way.

"So, we're going home?"

The place he hadn't been able to make himself set foot in since he blew his own world to pieces. Even the idea of it had nausea setting up in his gut. But alongside the queasiness was a kernel of desperate hope because this disaster meant that, like it or not, he'd finally see Abbey again.

Kyle shoved out the door. "We're going home."

Mom: **On the way! Thanks for everything!**

"Okay, my parents are officially on the road," Abbey announced. "Everybody, pray." Despite all the friends who'd agreed to help, she had no real backup if something went wrong, so she needed the next ten days to go smoothly.

Taryn Washington leaned one generous hip against the spa's front desk. "Well, I think it's just the nicest thing you're doing for your folks."

"Seriously," Nadia Flores agreed. "I wish somebody would send me on a cruise."

Abbey shrugged. "They've been through a lot. If this senior care program works, it will make a big difference to everybody's quality of life. His dementia isn't too bad yet, but he can't stay alone for long stretches anymore. We're trying to keep things as normal as possible for him, and that's just taken a lot out of us. We all need a break."

Pru Reynolds Bohannon, Abbey's friend and business partner, squeezed her shoulder. "I've been hearing good things."

A timer sounded on Taryn's watch. "That's the end of the foot-soak. Anybody got time to help me out with this mother-daughter mani-pedi?"

"I don't have anybody for another hour, and it'll give me a chance to sit down. I'm in." Abbey followed her into the treatment room.

Like the rest of the spa, the shiplap walls were painted a soft, soothing gray. The women in the pedicure chairs were so clearly related, sharing the same hazel eyes and heart-shaped faces. Hailing from somewhere in Kentucky, they'd come in for a girl's trip yesterday and seemed to be having the time of their lives. Mom's head was tipped back, eyes closed as she relaxed with her feet in the warm water. Daughter poured over her phone.

As Abbey and Taryn walked in, the girl's eyes widened with shock, and she reached over blindly to pat at her mother's arm. "Oh, my God! I can't believe it."

"What is it?" her mother asked.

"Kyle Keenan is *engaged.* It's all over social media."

Mom laughed. "Well, there goes your diabolical plan to meet him after a show and make him fall madly in love with you."

All the air was promptly sucked from the room.

Kyle was engaged?

In the ensuing moments of shock, Abbey stood rooted to the spot, trying to remember how to breathe.

Taryn stepped into her line of sight, her smooth bronze face set in lines of sympathy and understanding. "Didn't you need to go prep for your next client?"

Not even able to speak, Abbey just bobbed

her head in a nod and did an about-face, her limbs jerking like a marionette. She strode across the building to her own treatment room, pushing the door mostly closed for an iota of privacy. Shutting it all the way would give this too much importance.

Kyle was *engaged.*

The breath she'd been holding wheezed out. Why should the idea of that upset her? He wasn't a part of her life anymore. They were less than friends now. Of course he'd moved on. But none of that stopped the mental video of the day he'd proposed with that candy machine ring.

They'd been hanging upside down from the branch of one of the apple trees way out in the west orchard, seeing who could stand the blood rushing to their head the longest. He'd dropped first, landing in a heap of gangly little boy limbs. "You win!"

She'd collapsed beside him, doing a double fist-pump before wrapping her arm around his skinny shoulders. "Hang on to me. I'll keep you steady."

They'd flopped back in the grass, his head on her shoulder, staring up at a blue sky studded with cotton-candy clouds as they waited for the world to stop spinning.

"I been thinkin', you're my best friend, Abs."

"Duh." They'd always been best friends. They always would be.

"Your granddaddy says you should marry your best friend."

"It worked out for him and Grandma Ruth," she'd agreed.

"We should get married."

As she'd decided on that months ago, when they'd watched *Aladdin*, she was amenable. But even at six, she'd been practical. "We can't get married yet, silly. We're too young."

"When we're older, then. How about when we turn twenty-one? That's forever away."

"It's the official grown-up age." Mama and Daddy said so.

"So, it's settled. We'll get married when we're twenty-one."

"Okay."

He sat up, and so did she, each staring at the other with as much gravity as children could muster. Then they'd spat into the palms of their hands and shaken on it—the most serious of promises. Kyle had nodded at that and pulled something out of his pocket.

"I got this for you."

It was a plastic ring, the kind that had come out of the candy machine down at Garden of Eden, the market in town. It might as well have been the crown jewels. The gesture spoke of forethought and intent, and she'd fallen in love with him then and there— insofar as a six-year-old was capable of such things. She'd kept that silly ring for years, a part of her foolishly believing that they'd both meant the promise they'd made that day.

He hadn't. That had been the end of it. The end of them as... anything.

He was a grown man. A rising success. He

had everything he always wanted. Of course, he'd have found someone by now. It was fine. Maybe him being taken would kill off the tiny, idiotic part of her that thought he'd someday come back to honor that spit shake, no matter how things had ended between them. The part that believed there was anything left of the man he used to be in the man he'd become.

"I'm looking for Abbey."

The sound of her name had her shoving her reaction aside. She'd wasted enough time and energy on Kyle Keenan. There was work to be done. Scrubbing both hands over her face and slipping on a mask of professionalism, she stepped out of her treatment room.

Nadia was talking to a man she didn't recognize. He didn't look like their usual clients. His patchy beard seemed more like the result of not bothering to shave for weeks, rather than growing one on purpose, and she was pretty sure that streak of neon orange stuff down the front of his sweater was dust from a bag of Cheetos. Maybe a client had recommended her services? Or maybe he wanted to buy a gift card for someone else?

"Can I help you?"

The guy had a weird intensity about him that made her uncomfortable. His gaze seemed full of a manic glitter, his smile just a shade too bright.

"Oh, I've come a long way to find you."

What the actual hell?

The door opened again, and she glanced toward it, hoping Pru's husband, Flynn, was popping in as well-timed backup. Then she did a double take because a ghost walked in.

He was older, his shoulders a little broader than they'd been at twenty-one. His cheeks had long ago lost the last roundness of youth and now sported a close-cropped blond beard highlighting a very adult jaw. His vivid blue eyes met hers, and there was no stopping the electric current of hope and joy beneath the jolt of shock.

"Kyle?" She hated the breathless quality of her voice, but she couldn't look away from the answering joy and blinding smile. He was a very vivid hallucination. The news of his engagement had broken something in her overtaxed brain.

He crossed the distance between them in a few long-legged strides, and then his hands were sliding into her hair. "Missed you," he rasped and took her mouth with his.

Oh, yeah, she'd definitely passed out and had some kind of head injury. Because no way in hell was her ex-best friend kissing the bejeezus out of her like she'd always wanted him to. Like he was drowning, and she was oxygen. Like they hadn't spent the past decade not speaking, and he hadn't shattered her heart. He only ever did that in dreams because the privacy of her own mind was the only place she could still be honest.

And if she was dreaming, then it was safe to indulge in the fantasy.

CHAPTER 3

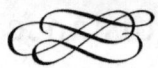

*K*yle had no plan.

They'd driven hell for leather to get here, only to walk in and see her standing in the lobby with Howie Frick, one of the cretinous paparazzi who haunted the country music scene. He'd thought for sure he was already too late. But then Abbey had seen him, and her first reaction hadn't been anger or hurt. She'd looked... happy to see him. After how things had ended between them, that was the last thing he'd expected. In that moment, kissing her had seemed like the smartest, most vital thing in the world.

He'd gone in prepared for her to push him away, maybe try to slap him. Her little purr of surrender wrecked all thoughts of giving Griff time to hustle Howie out the door. As she rose against him, pressing closer, Kyle forgot everything else but the woman in his arms— the one he'd dreamed about, sang of, and pined over for more than ten long years. The one who was undeniably kissing him back. Her mouth opened under his, and he swept deeper, desperate to fill the void in his chest with the taste of her. Why the hell hadn't they been doing this every day for years? Nothing else mattered but that he never, ever let her go again.

The rapid-fire click of a camera shutter brought him back.

Camera. Paparazzi. Audience. Shit.

Lifting his head only far enough to speak, he growled one word. "Griff."

"On it."

"Hey! That's my camera!"

"And this is private property."

"It's a public business!"

"Do we need to have another conversation about what is and is not appropriate behavior?"

Kyle didn't need to look to know Griff was hauling the guy out. It wasn't the first time.

He kept his eyes on Abbey's face, his hands still woven into the silk of her hair. Her lips were pink and swollen from his, and the soft, stunned expression in her big, brown eyes was fading, replaced by... well, he didn't know what, but they needed to get somewhere private fast before her brain kicked back online.

Wrapping an arm around her shoulders, he hustled Abbey toward the nearest open room and shut the door behind them. The moment he did, she jerked away, whirling on him.

"What the actual hell?" This was the furious woman he'd been braced for.

"Keep your voice down."

"Give me one good reason why."

"You kissed me back." Not exactly the kind of reason she was asking for, but it was the detail his brain was spotlighting.

She opened her mouth as if to refute him and then closed it again. Her cheeks suffused with color, and her hands curled into fists. "You're engaged!" she hissed.

Christ, he hadn't considered she could hear about part without hearing about the whole. He lifted his hands in peace. "To you!"

"To... What?" Profound shock replaced the fury.

Yeah, okay, she hadn't expected that. Wishing he'd thought this through and that he had any blood flow to his brain, he struggled to find the words. "I can explain."

"Talk. Fast."

"I might have accidentally let it slip this morning during a live interview that we were engaged."

Her brows climbed even further toward her hairline. "Might have?"

"Okay, I sort of did," he conceded. Did the

fact that it hadn't been on purpose make it better or worse?

"Are you out of your mind?"

Someone knocked softly and opened the door. His foster sister, Pru, stepped inside. "I'm sorry to interrupt... whatever this is, but the elder care is on the phone, Abbey. They've been trying to reach you."

She bolted from the room without a backward glance.

Pru crossed her arms and somehow managed to stare down her nose at him, despite being several inches shorter.

Kyle rubbed the back of his neck. "Hey, sis."

"Don't you 'Hey, sis' me. You stay away from home all these years and now you come into my place of business like this, doing—" She waved a finger toward the lobby. "—whatever the heck that was. You've got more than a little explaining to do."

He'd seen all of them at their brother Caleb's wedding last fall, but he understood that wasn't enough. Not when he'd missed the family reunion and Joan's funeral before that. "That's completely fair. And I promise I will, but I need to talk to Abbey first."

He started for the door, but Pru stepped into his path. "I hope you two sort things out. It's way past overdue. But if you hurt her again, I'll string you up myself."

He wondered how much she knew. "Yes, ma'am."

This time, she didn't stop him when he moved past her. He stepped into the lobby just in time to see all the blood drain out of Abbey's face.

"I'm on my way." It took her two tries to get the phone hung up. She lifted huge, terrified eyes to him.

No, not to him. To Pru, who'd skirted around him.

"Honey, what's wrong?"

"Granddaddy had a fall and got hurt. They called an ambulance. He's on his way to the hospital in Johnson City."

Kyle's own hands clenched with the need

to do something... anything. This was a man who'd once treated him as family. Who'd taught him how to whittle wood. How to peel an apple in one long strip. He had to be okay.

"Oh my God. Go. We'll cover everything here," Pru insisted.

Abbey yanked open a drawer in the front desk and grabbed her purse. "Where the hell are my keys?" She pawed through it for several long moments.

When she made as if to upend the entire bag, Kyle moved in to stop her, laying his hands over hers. He could feel the tremors running through her. "I'll drive."

He knew it was bad when she didn't even try to argue.

Griff came back inside. "Frick's gone. Not sure for how long, but I think I bought you at least a few days with my creative threats of where I'd shove his camera if I saw his ugly mug here again."

"Need keys."

Without hesitation, Griff tossed them over.

Glancing back at Pru, he said, "I'll explain later. Just… if anybody shows up asking about me… or Abbey, put them off and tell them nothing."

Pressing a hand to Abbey's lower back, he led her out to his SUV. As they stepped out the door, he could hear Pru. "Apparently, it's the day for homecomings. Welcome back, Griffin."

Griff would be fine. The family would take care of him while he did this. It's what all of them who'd spent time at The Misfit Inn before it had been turned into a literal inn had been raised to do. The family you made stuck.

Abbey said nothing as they climbed into the Land Cruiser. Her breaths were quick and shallow, her hands knotted in white-knuckled fists in her lap as he headed for Johnson City.

"Why is Griff with you?"

"He finished his stint in the Marines a few months ago. I hired him as security on my tour."

"Oh."

They lapsed back into silence for a while. It wasn't one of the easy silences they'd shared in their youth. It was full of emotional landmines, past and present, and Kyle hardly knew where to step.

"Do you need to call your folks?"

She pressed the heels of both hands to her eyes. "My parents just left for a ten-day cruise this morning. I sent them for their anniversary. I told them I could handle him on my own. And now…"

He hated the self-recrimination in her voice. "What's going on with Granddaddy other than this fall?"

"He has dementia. We think it started after Grandma Ruth passed a few years ago. He has long stretches of good days, and because he's worked the orchards his whole life, we missed the signs for a while. But eventually, we couldn't deny what was happening. A couple years ago, he ran the tractor into the side of the barn because he forgot to set the brake. It was a miracle he wasn't hurt and that nobody else was either. I moved home after that to help take care of him."

This was all stuff Kyle should have known. These people had once been family. But, of course, no one had told him. Why would they? He'd screwed things up and hadn't been a part of their lives. Not even enough for his sisters to keep him up to date. The guilt over that was a bitter taste in his mouth.

Before he could express his regrets—he had so damned many when it came to this woman—Abbey was speaking again.

"So… what is this whole engaged thing?"

He glanced over at her, glad to see a trace of color back in her cheeks. "We don't have to talk about this right now."

"You brought this to my doorstep, and it's a distraction to keep me from freaking out right now. Why in the hell did you say we were engaged?"

"My manager and my label have been pressuring me to hook up with Mercy Lee Bradshaw for publicity purposes. There's no amount of money or publicity on earth that would induce me to do that, so I figured I'd shut that shit down by announcing I was promised to someone else. I didn't mean to mention your name, but I kinda got tricked into it. Combination of no sleep and a sneaky host."

There went the eyebrow again, but she let that pass. "Why me?"

One corner of his mouth twitched into a smile. "I mean, technically, you're the only woman I've ever been engaged to."

"We were six."

"I still meant it."

On a disbelieving snort, she turned to look out the window. "Maybe you did back then."

"Abbey, I—"

"No." The single word stopped him more effectively than a slap.

Right. This was not about fixing things between them. This was about distraction from whatever was waiting for her at the hospital.

"I didn't mean to dump this on you."

"It's your mess. You can clean it up. Issue a retraction or... whatever."

The idea had a fresh spate of panic bursting through him. He didn't want to announce it had been a lie. For better or worse, she was talking to him right now for the first time in forever. If he could keep it that way, maybe he could prove to her he wasn't who she thought he'd become.

"It's not that simple."

"Sure it is. You open your mouth to say that you didn't mean it or the host misinterpreted or whatever. Then you go back to your life, and I go back to mine."

"That isn't going to stop the paparazzi from harassing you."

"I'm nobody. None of them are going to care about me."

"Unfortunately, yeah they will, because of me."

"Then I'll set them straight."

"The gossip rags likely already have their teeth in this. They're going to run with whatever story they think plays best. You won't get left alone if I just publicly announce 'Oops, my bad.'"

"So, what are you going to do about it?"

"I don't know yet. My top priority was getting here to tell you before someone else had the chance. I'll get my publicist on it." Deanna was probably going on the growing list of people who wanted to kosh him over the head with a blunt instrument. She and Abbey would get along great.

He pulled up to the doors of the Emergency Department with no little relief. "Right now, the only thing that matters is Granddaddy. Go on in. Find out what's going on. I'll park and come find you."

Abbey slid out of the front seat, shooting him a confused glance. "Thanks for driving me." She hesitated, one hand on the door. "This doesn't mean you're forgiven."

"I didn't think it would."

But as she shut the door and strode into the hospital, he wondered if his big fat mouth might have just given him the perfect excuse to get close enough to her to earn that for-giveness.

"THE GOOD NEWS: Nothing's broken. You're incredibly lucky, Mr. Whittaker."

Abbey let go of the breath she'd been holding since the doctor, a studious-looking black man in wire-framed glasses, came back to their little curtained-off exam room. That was one prayer answered.

"The bad news: You've rolled your ankle badly. The inflammation is pretty nasty, and you'll be unstable on your feet for a while. You're going to need to keep off it. Elevation, ice, crutches. Do you have someone who can stay with you to help out?"

"I live with him. I'll be there," Abbey in-terjected.

"There's no need for that. You've got work."

"Mr. Whittaker, you might not be so lucky with another fall," Dr. Johnson warned. "And at your age and condition, a broken hip or a head injury could be—well, let's not go there, shall we?"

Abbey heard what he didn't say. Another fall could lead to an injury that would be a death sentence. Granddaddy didn't understand his own fragility as a dementia patient, but she did. The next ten days without her parents just gotten infinitely more complicated. "We'll work everything out." She didn't know how, but right now she couldn't think past getting home.

That was when she remembered she hadn't driven herself. Kyle had brought her. It said a lot about how worried she'd been that she'd managed to block out that detail for the last few hours. Was he still here? Maybe he called back to the inn and traded off with… someone else. She could hope. She didn't know how she was going to handle the ride all the way back to Eden's Ridge. If she wasn't driving, she'd have time to think, and that was a dangerous proposition.

It was, of course, Kyle himself who rose from a seat in the Emergency Department waiting room, when they emerged from the back. Much as she'd painted him with a villain's brush over the past ten years, she'd known he wouldn't just leave her with no way to get home. He'd seemed just as concerned about Granddaddy as she was on the drive over.

"Everything all right?" He'd donned a baseball cap and some Clark Kent glasses that almost made her smile at the cheesiness.

"Bunch of fuss for nothin'," Granddaddy insisted from his wheelchair. "Just a sprain. I could've walked it off."

Kyle eyed the crutches Abbey carried. "Doesn't look like you're gonna be walking for a little while, either way."

Granddaddy crossed his arms and scowled. "Well, I suppose you'll get extra time on the tractor this week. But don't you let it interfere with your schoolwork, Kyle."

Of course, he'd recognize Kyle after all these years. It seemed he was also stuck in the amber of high school, as she so often was for her grandfather.

Kyle's sharp blue gaze flicked to her and back to Granddaddy. "No, sir."

When he lagged a few steps, Abbey dropped back herself. "He slips in and out of the past. Sometimes he thinks I'm still in high school. Sometimes he thinks I'm Grandma Ruth. We try to humor him as much as possible because arguing about when it is or who we are just upsets him. Most of the time, he comes out of it on his own."

Kyle nodded once, shoving the glasses up the bridge of his nose.

Abbey couldn't quite hold back a smirk. "Does that getup actually work as a disguise?"

One corner of his mouth lifted in a rueful smile. "You'd be surprised."

They trailed the nurse to the entrance, and

Abbey waited with her grandfather until Kyle brought the Land Cruiser around. They got him settled in the backseat, with his ankle propped up. After a brief stop at a drive-thru for fast-food burgers, they headed toward home. She fought not to stare as the two of them slid into easy conversation, like it hadn't been years since they'd seen each other.

When it became readily apparent her contribution wasn't needed, Abbey blew out a breath and relaxed for the first time since she'd gotten the call. For all intents and purposes, her grandfather was okay. His injury wasn't life threatening. It hadn't required surgery or an overnight stay in the hospital. And that was good. She already wasn't sure how much the ambulance ride was going to set them back. But an overnight would have required she contact her parents, and she didn't want to ruin their trip. More, she didn't want to be proved incapable when she'd insisted he'd be fine with her. They were out of port by now, so she had to make this work.

She'd need to cancel appointments for at least the next couple of days. She couldn't possibly ask Pru to let her bring him to work at the spa. It wasn't everybody else's responsibility to keep an eye on him to make sure he stayed off that foot. The medical costs, on top of the chunk she'd dropped to pay for the cruise, was going to hurt. But she'd do what needed doing. For now, the focus had to be on what was right in front of her.

She began mulling over what accommodations needed to be made for his current condition. They'd been talking about converting the downstairs study into a bedroom for him for a while, as his balance had gotten to be more of an issue. No way did she want him trying to manage stairs on crutches. So that would need to be flipped.

"It's gotta be the '65," Granddaddy insisted.

"It's a sexy car, I admit. But the '69 and '70 is where it's at. Speed, class, and that engine, man. You can't beat it."

This man chatting with her grandfather so

much resembled the boy she'd loved and not what she was expecting. Abbey shook her head in silent denial as the bitterness washed through her. How the hell did she get here, being chauffeured from the hospital by her best friend turned enemy? A man she'd done her best to despise. To forget. A man she'd kissed as she did in the dreams she admitted to only in the dark of night. Abbey's cheeks heated at the memory. So did the rest of her. Thank God the sun had long gone down so no one could see.

In all her thousands of imagined scenarios for when she saw him again, she'd never imagined any of this. There'd been groveling. Serenading. Heart-felt confessions. A great many of those situations had ended with a slap because, even ten years on, she couldn't forgive him for the things he'd said.

God, how could she have kissed him back? The truth was, as many years as she'd been harboring the hurt, she still wanted him, and her inner teen girl, who'd been in love with her best friend since time immemorial, had flat-out swooned because she'd wanted his kiss for years. But not as some kind of act. Not as a cover story. She'd wanted him to want her. To choose her.

He hadn't, when it mattered. And now he'd gone and announced they were engaged in a live interview. She still couldn't quite believe he'd done that. But that paparazzi guy had showed up at the spa, and what else would have dragged Kyle home after all these years? She didn't think he'd lied about saying it. It would be too easy to verify, which she should probably do to see *what* had been said.

Why her? What did it say that hers was the name he blurted out on impulse? That he'd been thinking of her? Of that silly ring and that day in the orchard?

The whole thing gave her a headache. It would have to be sorted out tomorrow.

Kyle drove them straight home. Probably for the best. She didn't think it would be easy to get Granddaddy transferred from the SUV to her little car. The fewer unnecessary moves, the better.

He tried to get out on his own as soon as they rolled to a stop.

"Wait, wait. Let me get your crutches." Abbey leapt out.

"I don't need any damned crutches," Granddaddy insisted.

"How about using me for one?" Kyle suggested, ducking under his arm. "It'll make the womenfolk happy."

"Well, all right then."

Abbey pressed her lips together to keep from commenting as she trailed them up the porch steps and into the house. Kyle got him settled in the recliner in the den.

"There. You're the official king of the castle in that chair. And your humble servant will get you some ice." He sketched a bow and turned toward the kitchen.

Abbey stared after him, dumbstruck at his ability to just walk in here like it hadn't been years. She heard the freezer door. A minute later he came back with a bag of frozen peas and a kitchen towel.

"I expect we can sacrifice some peas in the name of an ice pack. This should mold to your ankle a little better." Gently, he settled the peas in place.

"Thanks, son."

Kyle straightened and caught her still staring. He handed Granddaddy the remote and jerked his head toward the kitchen. "Talk to you for a minute?"

Because she couldn't think what else to do, she trailed him out of the room.

In the kitchen, he turned, eyes searching her face. "You okay, Abs?"

No. She was not anywhere in the vicinity of okay. She didn't know how to handle being here, in this house, with Kyle. Just below the surface, emotions were set to hit a rolling boil, and she didn't know what would happen when they spilled over.

But she wasn't about to tell him that. "I was just trying to figure out the logistics of how we're going to get my car. I can't leave Grand-daddy alone to go get it."

"I'll drive you to get it when we get up in the morning."

"What the hell are you talking about?"

"I'm staying to help. With your folks gone, I expect you could use a hand."

She absolutely could. But not *him.*

Keeping her voice low, she prowled toward him. "You've been out of my life for years, and now you're just sliding in and acting like everything hasn't changed?"

He sucked in a breath, and she thought he might've been counting to ten. "Look, I brought a mess and more stress to your doorstep. The least I can do is help you out with this. You can argue with me about it to-morrow after you've had some sleep, and we're sure everything is copacetic with Granddaddy. I'm guessing we need to do some kind of switcharoo with furniture so he can sleep down here tonight?"

She could keep arguing. But it didn't

change the fact that he was right. She couldn't move the bed on her own, and she didn't want Granddaddy's old bones to suffer on the fold-out in the living room.

"Fine. You can stay the night, and we'll sort out the rest in the morning."

"All right. Let's go move a bed." He started toward the stairs.

"Kyle."

When he turned back, a question on his face, Abbey pressed her lips together for a long moment. "Thank you for being here today."

Something that might've been pain flashed in his eyes before he dropped his gaze in a nod. Without another word, he trotted up the stairs.

Sucking in a bracing breath, she followed.

CHAPTER 4

*K*yle woke to silence. For long moments, he lay still, eyes closed, trying to orient himself. There was no sense of motion from sleeping on the bus. None of the city noises he'd grown accustomed to on the road. He heard none of the muted sounds of Nashville traffic from his loft. Cracking his eyes, he registered he was on a sofa, in a house he hadn't seen in more years than he cared to count.

The farm.

Abbey.

Rolling to his back, he scrubbed both hands over his face, and his whole body twinged from wedging his six-foot frame onto too short a couch. Abbey had offered him a guest room, but he'd opted for the sofa in case Granddaddy needed something in the night because he figured if he didn't, she would, and she'd looked ready to drop last night. Besides, after all these years on the road, he'd trained himself to sleep wherever, whenever he could.

He sat up, shoving off the quilt and scooping a hand through his hair as he took in the room he hadn't paid much attention to last night. He recognized Grandma Ruth's painting of the east orchard hanging above the mantle. The built-in bookcases on either side were still stuffed to bursting with a hodge-podge of books and family photos. There were new slipcovers on the chairs that flanked the fireplace, and it looked like they'd picked up some new end tables to go with the newer sofa where he'd spent his night. But even with the changes, even after all these years, this place still felt like home in a way nowhere else ever had. Not that he'd stayed anywhere else long enough to make what would constitute a home. His loft didn't quite count since he was so often on tour.

Gray dawn light told him it was early. Scenting coffee, he pulled on his T-shirt and followed his nose to the kitchen. Grabbing a mug from the cabinet by the sink, he poured himself a cup and enjoyed the first hit of caffeinated steam, knowing he didn't have to race to be anywhere, do anything. Sipping at the scalding black brew, he wandered out to the front porch to watch as the sun rose over the same orchards in Grandma Ruth's painting. Gooseflesh rose along his arms from the chill morning air, but he didn't go back inside. Unfamiliar peace wrapped around him, soothing jagged edges. Something in him realigned and settled at the sight. As if he'd been out of phase with himself until this moment. It wasn't so far from the truth.

"Surprised you're up."

Kyle didn't jolt at the sound of Abbey's voice. Maybe a part of him had known she'd be out here. He looked over to find her wrapped in a thick gray sweater and blanket, in one of the wicker chairs that lined the front porch. Her blonde hair was pulled into a messy tail that trailed over one shoulder, and her big, doe eyes were still heavy from sleep as she blinked at him over her own steaming mug. A melody began to unfurl in his brain as he took her in, and his fingers itched for a pen and paper.

"Granddaddy okay?" he asked.

"Still sleeping. But that probably won't last much longer. He's usually up with the sun."

Kyle grunted and sipped more coffee, forcing himself to look away from her toward the land he'd once loved more than anywhere else in the world. It was more run down than he remembered. Some sagging eaves here, peeling paint there. Guilt prickled at that. Had they struggled? Were things worse than he'd realized after his parents went to prison? He didn't feel like he could ask. Not now.

Abbey shoved up from her chair. "I need to call into work. No way can Granddaddy go back to senior care today."

"I can stay with him." The offer was out before the caffeine hit his brain, but Kyle didn't want to retract it.

She was back to looking at him like he'd grown a second head. "What?"

He jerked his shoulders, sipped more coffee. "I don't have anywhere I need to be. I'm done with the tour."

Her brows drew together. "Why would you do that?"

It grated that they'd reached a point where such an offer surprised her. "Because you need help, and I'm here. Because he's the closest thing I ever had to a grandfather. Because once upon a time, we were family."

A flash of something—Hurt? Temper?—flickered over her face. She opened her mouth to say something, but a shouted, "Dagnabbit!" from inside announced that Granddaddy was up, and she swallowed whatever it was back down.

Without answering, she went inside. For a few more minutes, Kyle stayed where he was, wondering what he'd have to do to convince her to talk about what had happened between them. He figured he could start by making himself useful. By the time Abbey helped Granddaddy into the kitchen, Kyle had bacon sizzling and eggs ready to go into a skillet.

"Lotta fuss for nothing. It's just a little twingy."

"It will be a lot worse than a little twingy if you don't stay off it like the doctor said. Sit. I'll fix your coffee." Abbey installed him in a kitchen chair and crossed to the coffeepot.

Kyle felt her gaze on him at the stove, but figured it was better to pretend all was normal. He wasn't sure what frame of mind Granddaddy was in this morning. Removing the bacon, he drained off the excess grease and dumped in the eggs.

"Smells good," Granddaddy declared. "You draft your boyfriend as short-order cook this morning?"

Boyfriend? Shit, *did* Abbey have a boyfriend? In all the chaos yesterday, he'd never asked. He hadn't even considered the possibility.

Abbey made a choking noise.

Carrying the plate of bacon to the table, Kyle kept his tone easy. "Nah, I figured cooking breakfast was the least I could do for y'all putting me up last night."

The old man's eyes narrowed. Did he recognize him? "Well damn, you grew up."

Kyle laughed. "Sure did. Good to see you, sir."

"Oh, don't sir me, boy. And mind those eggs don't burn."

He moved back to the stove, wondering how much Granddaddy remembered of the hospital last night.

"Need to hurry on up. I've gotta drive

down to the feed and farm supply to pick up our order this morning."

Even without the injured ankle, Kyle was pretty sure he shouldn't be driving, a fact confirmed by a quick glance at Abbey.

"Actually, I figured we'd have some lessons in how to use those crutches. I've got more practice than you. If you need to go somewhere today, I'll drive you. You can give me the grand tour and show me everything that's changed, while Abbey's at work."

"You don't have to—" she began.

"Sounds good! Lots of catching up to do. Can't say I'll mind having a younger back to load things."

Kyle slid the bowl of eggs onto the table and met Abbey's gaze. "It'd be my pleasure."

Her eyes were ripe with distrust. For a moment, he thought she'd refuse out of stubborn principle. Then her lips flattened. "Thank you, I appreciate it."

The tone was grudging, but it wasn't a no, so he'd take it. "We'll finish breakfast and load all of us up. Granddaddy and I can drop you at the inn so you'll have your car."

Oh, she hated needing him for anything. Her nostrils flared with frustration at the situation, but again, she only nodded and shoved back from the table. "Then I'd best clean up and get ready to go."

"You didn't eat," Kyle pointed out.

"Not hungry."

He could hear the pique in her steps as she went upstairs to shower.

When the banging pipes signaled she'd retreated into the bathroom, Granddaddy lifted his coffee and surveyed Kyle over the rim of his mug. "Well, took you long enough to come home."

He paused with a forkful of eggs halfway to his mouth. "Sorry?"

"You should be. Don't know what happened between you two, but it's long past time for you to fix it. The whole damned situation's been festering for years. So what's the plan?"

"I don't… have one?" A plan would indicate

he had a damned clue what he was doing, rather than fumbling his way in the dark.

"That's just damned foolishness, and you done used up your quota, son. You ain't gonna win her back without being tactical. My granddaughter's a Whittaker. Stubborn as they come."

Granddaddy was a lot more with it than Abbey had led him to believe, and it sounded like he was on Kyle's side. Kyle didn't know what to do with that.

When he only continued to stare, Granddaddy arched a bushy brow. "What? I know I've got memory problems, son, but I've never been blind to how you feel about my granddaughter. You've been stupid in love with her since you were knee high."

Kyle was too stuck on the first thing Granddaddy had said to be flustered at being called out for the feelings he hadn't fully admitted to anyone. "You think I have a shot at winning her back? Or, hell, winning her in the first place?"

"You won her years ago. You just have to remind her."

He glanced up at the ceiling, where he could hear muffled strains of what sounded like "You Better Think" by Aretha Franklin. "I don't think it'll be that simple."

"Love never is. But it's worth the work. Now let's make a plan."

THE MOMENT KYLE'S SUV pulled up to the Misfit Inn and Spa, Abbey opened the door and slid out. She needed to escape his orbit for the sake of her sanity.

"Have a good day, Abbey."

She shot him a level look. "I'm trusting you to behave yourselves." She'd given him a full list of dos and don'ts for Granddaddy before they left the house.

He saluted from the driver's seat. "I won't let you down."

They'd see about that.

"You've got my number if anything happens." God help her.

"I'll take good care of Granddaddy." There was no trace of cocky amusement in his tone or expression, and she could only hope she'd properly conveyed the seriousness of the situation.

Abbey opened the door to the backseat and ducked in to brush a kiss over Granddaddy's wrinkled cheek. "You behave, too. Don't overdo on that ankle."

"Fine, fine. I'll be good."

Kyle shut off the engine and slid out of the driver's seat.

Abbey's heart kicked up as he circled around toward her. "What are you doing?"

"We're just gonna grab Griff while we're here and sort out transportation."

Oh right, they'd come together.

Jerking her head in a quick nod, she backed away, lifting her hand in a last wave to her grandfather. Sending up a prayer, she turned her back on them both and strode into the spa.

She'd made them leave the house way early, hoping she'd beat everyone to work and get some time and space to clear her head and figure out what to say. The sprawl of figures around the beverage station made it clear she'd have no respite. At least it was only Pru's sister, Kennedy, who'd wandered over from the inn for the inquisition.

Pru shot out of a chair. "How is your grandfather?"

On a slow exhale of breath, Abbey dropped her purse. "He's okay. A badly sprained ankle, but things could have been so much worse. He'll be on crutches and need to stay off it a while."

Nadia offered her a mug of coffee. "We weren't sure if we needed to cancel your appointments."

"For now, no. Kyle's keeping an eye on him. He stayed at the farm last night after bringing us back from the hospital." At the assortment of raised brows, she added. "On the sofa." Ignoring the wide, expectant eyes, Abbey sipped at the coffee.

When she said nothing, Pru prodded, "And is there... something else you want to tell us?"

Abbey opted to play dumb. "About?"

"Girl!" Taryn exploded. "How 'bout what is up with that fine specimen of a man whose guts you have pretended to hate for years coming up in here and laying one on you?"

"Oh. That." She clutched the mug like a shield and winced. "Is it too early to day drink?"

Kennedy crossed her arms. "Is this a mimosa or tequila sort of situation?"

"Definitely tequila." A pitcher of margaritas would go a long way toward making her forget about yesterday. Maybe.

"How long have you two been seeing each other?" Pru's tone was carefully neutral, betraying none of the I-am-your-best-friend-how-could-you-not-tell-me she had to be feeling.

Abbey's laugh held an edge of hysteria. "Yesterday is the first time I've seen him in a decade."

"But that kiss..."

Wishing for that tequila shot, Abbey just shook her head. "I don't know what to say about that."

"I do. That was hot," Nadia proclaimed.

She'd been trying hard not to think about. Not that her dreams had gotten the message. The whole thing had played in glorious Technicolor repeat last night, with a multitude of different endings that hadn't involved an audience or interruption by skeezy photographers. She'd woken early, hot and restless and needy. A situation not at all helped by the sight of him sleeping shirtless on the living room sofa this morning. Just the memory of the smooth expanse of his chest and the golden trail of hair that disappeared beneath Grandma Ruth's quilt had heat blooming in her cheeks.

Her friends smirked.

"I didn't realize you and he..." Pru trailed off.

Kennedy snorted with disbelief. "Really? I did. I've been expecting this for years. And I wasn't even in the country for most of them."

"Can we address the elephant in the room? The man is supposed to be engaged," Taryn pointed out.

Stunned silence gave way to a babble of voices as they all voiced their opinion of that situation.

Abbey pinched the bridge of her nose and closed her eyes. "To me."

"*What?*" Their chorus of shock echoed off the atrium ceiling.

"It's not what you think."

"Oh, this I gotta hear." Taryn settled in and mimed eating popcorn.

"He's been getting a lot of pressure to pair up with Mercy Lee Bradshaw. As a publicity thing, I guess. He was tired of his manager and label pushing that agenda, so when he got cornered in an interview yesterday, he blurted out that he was already engaged."

"Why to you?" Nadia asked.

Her brain conjured a picture of that bubble gum ring and a pretty spring day. She shrugged with more nonchalance than she felt. "We had a marriage pact when we were little."

"So, it's not real," Pru qualified.

"No. That—" Abbey waved her hand, unable to bring herself to reference the kiss. "—yesterday was cover. Apparently."

"But now everybody thinks you're engaged," Taryn pressed.

"I'm sure not everybody. One guy showed up." She couldn't imagine this being a big enough deal to be more than a blip.

"Um... not just one," Pru said. "Four more materialized before the end of the day. We all played dumb like Kyle asked, but I don't think that's going to be the end of it."

Abbey could only stare. How could this be such a thing?

"Maybe we should check to see exactly what's out there." Kennedy moved to the computer at the registration desk and pulled up a browser. Her fingers flew over the keys. A few mouse clicks later she whistled. "You're going to want to see this."

Abbey circled around to the computer. The image hit her straight in the face. For a moment, the only thing she could see were her hands fisted in Kyle's shirt, her body plastered to his. Nothing about her body language in that picture supported her position that she was still hurt and furious with him. Then her gaze skimmed up to the bold headline at the top.

Has Country Music's Captain America found his Peggy?

"This is already everywhere. Abbey, they have your name."

"Oh, my god." Knees going weak, she gripped the back of the chair.

This insanity was only just beginning.

CHAPTER 5

The feed and farm supply hadn't changed much since Kyle left Eden's Ridge. Scents of earth and leather and gardening chemicals slapped him in the face as he stepped inside the tin-roofed building behind Granddaddy, bringing to mind countless trips here from childhood and, later, his teen years. The black man behind the counter had a little more gray in his close-cropped hair, but his booming voice was still the same as he called out, "What the heck happened to you, Roy?"

Granddaddy crutched his way over to a chair near the register, where a cluster of other old-timers were lingering over little Styrofoam cups of black coffee. "It was the damnedest thing."

Stan came out from behind the register and brought him a cup of coffee himself. "Looks nasty. Is it broken?"

"By the grace of God, no."

Kyle smiled to himself as Granddaddy launched into the story. He understood that this was as much a social opportunity as a shopping trip. It was a rare stop here that was less than half an hour.

Beside him, Griff eyed the racks of clothes off to one side of the store. "Maybe we should pick up a few things. Unless you're planning to head back to Nashville today?"

"I don't know how long we'll be here."

"That's what I thought." He wandered off to pick out some jeans.

Kyle headed for a rack of Henleys. Leaving with no packed bag wasn't the smartest thing he'd ever done, but he hadn't wanted to slow down for anything yesterday. And good thing, too. Who knew what would have happened with Frick if he hadn't interrupted?

And that just made Kyle think about the kiss.

As angry as Abbey was—as distrustful as she was—her first response had been to kiss him back. An electric, desperate kiss that wiped away every hurt, every mile, every year. For just a little while. He'd spent years of their friendship ignoring the attraction because he didn't feel worthy of her. Hell, it was a big part of why he'd left. To make something of himself. Hadn't he been told throughout his childhood that he was worthless? None of that had ever mattered to Abbey, but it had mattered to him that he bring something more to their marriage than himself. And he had intended to marry her. Had packed his bags, ready to leave and meet her. And then—

"Kyle?"

Blinking back to the present, he turned toward the woman, a shirt in each hand. He didn't recognize the blonde, but he seldom recognized people who called his name. Bracing himself for fangirling, he schooled his features into the Nice Guy smile.

If it affected her at all, she didn't show it. She offered a wide, self-deprecatory smile that said she knew he had no idea who she was. "Cayla Black. We had geometry together back in high school."

He had dim memories of a studious girl with wavy blonde hair and dark-framed glasses, who sat a couple rows ahead of him and Abbey, and he understood that this wasn't a typical fan interaction. This was small-town social obligation. The kind of thing that he'd have dealt with before if he'd bothered to come home in the last ten years. Flipping his mental script, he relaxed a bit. "Of course. Good to see you. How've you been?"

Cayla waved a hand. "Oh, you know."

He didn't.

"I left home for several years. Came back

with my daughter and started an event planning business."

He waited for the ask. An autograph. An introduction to someone. A date. But she only stood there smiling, open and friendly, waiting for him to complete the other half of this social ritual. The idea left him more than a little off-kilter and scrambling for a normal-person response. "That's great. How old is she?"

"Five going on thirty. Her latest campaign is for a puppy. Like we have time for that level of chaos. But, I admit, she's wearing me down." She laughed at herself. It was a comfortable sound, not an awkward, cowed-by-his-celebrity giggle to fill the silence. "How have you been?"

The idea that she wasn't up on the tabloids was odd and very appealing. *You aren't in Nashville anymore, buddy boy.* "Oh, you know. Making it. I'm in town to visit family for a bit."

Cayla beamed. "Oh, that's wonderful. I'm sure the girls have missed you."

That she defaulted to his sisters rather than blood kin made him want to hug her in gratitude.

His phone rang. Just in case it was Abbey, he slipped it out to check the screen and found Deanna James instead. His publicist wasn't someone he could put off at this point.

"I'm sorry. I have to take this. It was good to see you, Cayla." Good to have a conversation that made him feel like a normal guy again.

As she walked away to continue her own shopping, he answered, "Hey, D."

"What the actual hell, Kyle? When were you going to tell me you were engaged? This is stuff I'm supposed to be managing."

And so it begins.

His manager was the one who'd have called to inform her. "Sorry about that. I fired Davis yesterday, so I'm still picking up the slack." He'd have to take care of his own shit again until he found someone new. That was going to be a production.

In the long, humming silence, he grabbed a couple pairs of jeans in his size off a display.

"Good riddance. He's an ass. But we still have a situation. That picture of you and your lady is all over the tabloids. Speculation abounds, and people are starting to dig."

Digging was the last thing he wanted. For himself or for Abbey.

"It's just going to blow up and get bigger. There's no putting this genie back in the bottle. You and Abbey—is that actually her name?"

"Yes."

"Y'all are going to need to do some public appearances and—"

Kyle cut her off. "Abbey's a private person. She doesn't want this."

"You're going to need to get ahead of this before the media takes the crumbs dribbled out by Davis and your label over the last several months and spins some kind of shit about a love triangle and you throwing Mercy Lee over for this woman."

A headache throbbed behind his left eye. He realized that this was his last moment to tell the truth. To admit his faux pas in the interview and correct the course of this ship. It was what a good man would do. But, hell, Abbey already believed the worst of him, and he didn't want to give up this one last chance to maybe repair what he'd broken between them.

"Let me talk to Abbey and see what she's willing to do. I'll get back to you."

"You know how this works, Kyle. We have to control the narrative."

"Understood. I'll let you know."

Before he could contemplate the wisdom of this particular course of action, his phone rang again. This time it was Caleb. Kyle wasn't keen on whatever his brother had to say about the situation, but he took the call, anyway.

"Hey, bro."

"You know, when you told me you had to cancel your visit to take care of some business, I did not imagine that business would involve producing an engagement out of thin air. You have something you wanna tell me?"

When in doubt, play dumb. "Not really."

"Come on, man. Engaged? To Abbey? I talked to her last fall, and she wasn't anywhere *close* to forgiving you. So unless you somehow found the time to fly back across country during the tour to have that conversation I've been saying y'all should have for *years*, I smell a rat."

"It's complicated."

"Uncomplicate it for me."

"I'm in Eden's Ridge."

"I gathered that much from the picture of the lip lock with Abbey that's flying around everywhere. That doesn't explain why everybody suddenly thinks you're headed for wedded bliss."

Kyle cast a glance around, making sure no one was in earshot. He lowered his voice. "I mentioned things in my last interview that got misinterpreted. I'm here trying to control the fallout."

"Uh huh. And is Abbey on board with this?"

He thought of her reluctant acceptance of his presence. "I mean, she's talking to me again, so that's something."

"Seriously? I don't even know a tenth of the details, and I can tell this is a bad idea."

"Yeah, well, it's where I am right now. I'm staying at the farm helping out while her parents are out of town."

"Do I wanna know how you wrangled that?"

"Probably not."

"Have you actually *talked* to her? About before?" Caleb didn't know what had happened between them, but he'd been around to deal with the aftermath.

"No. But I will. Listen, I need to get going. I'll touch base, soon. Give Emerson my love."

"I will. And Kyle... don't fuck this up."

"I don't plan to."

Griff materialized as he hung up. "Everything okay?"

"Okay might be stretching it. We'll figure it out."

They had to. The alternative wasn't something he was willing to contemplate.

WITH ONE LAST, cautious glance into the rearview mirror, Abbey turned onto the long, winding drive to home, feeling none of the usual pleasure at the moonlit rows of apple trees rolling past her windows. Excessive caffeine and a simmering temper were the only things keeping profound exhaustion at bay. Her quiet, simple life was over, and it was all Kyle's fault.

Pulling up to the house, she started to go inside in search of her quarry, but the echo of male laughter on the wind had her turning toward the barn. The ancient pickup truck was parked beneath the floodlight outside, hood up. She'd driven right by them. The full head of steam she had yet to vent was apparently making her blind.

Abbey stalked over, relieved to see that at least Granddaddy sat in a lawn chair, his foot propped on a five-gallon bucket as he supervised his assistant. Kyle was bent over, with his head under the hood. Her steps slowed a little as she took in the stretch of denim over his backside. It was a very fine backside, even with a filthy shop rag dangling from one pocket. Annoyed with herself for noticing, she slowed even further.

The two of them were clearly having a grand old time, debating... what was that? Some past Super Bowl game? Was Granddaddy having one of his slides into the past or was this one of those weird male discussions of past sporting events, as if they were matters of actual import?

"I like their chances at the playoffs." Kyle emerged from the engine, some tool in his hand and a smear of grease beneath one eye. "Okay, let's try it now."

He circled around and slid into the driver's seat, turning the key in the ignition. It rumbled to life and began to purr, no longer making the knocking noise Granddaddy had reported the other day.

"Hell yeah!" Kyle whooped. He shut off the truck and slid out to high five Granddaddy.

"Well done, son!"

They beamed at each other, and the whole interaction felt like a sucker punch—because this was the old Kyle. Her best friend. Not the asshat who'd stabbed her through the heart. Abbey couldn't merge the two sides of him in her mind.

"Well, I guess y'all have had a productive day."

Kyle turned, his triumphant expression dialing even brighter at the sight of her. "Hey, Abs."

That instant joy at her presence was another sucker punch that left her irritable and reeling.

His smile faded. "Granddaddy, you stay

put, I'm gonna run up to the house to check on supper before I put all these tools away."

He'd made food? Again. She'd assumed this morning was an aberration. Abbey tried to wrap her head around that as she followed Kyle into the house. The kitchen was full of rich, spicy scents from something in the slow cooker. She couldn't resist lifting the lid for a peek as he washed his hands. Red beans and rice. One of her favorites.

"You made dinner?"

"It didn't seem right you should have to cook after a long day at work. Longer even than you expected, I take it. I thought you'd be home an hour ago." There was concern rather than censure in his tone.

On a sigh, she leaned back against the counter. "My day has been a shit show. Reporters started calling the spa. Several more showed up and tried to camp out. Griff had to play bouncer inside, and Xander had to post a deputy on the premises all afternoon. This insanity is interfering with the normal conduct of our business because we're having to parse out whether someone is a legitimate client or the press. Oh, and I had to take the long way home, just in case one of these lunatics tried to follow me."

His expression grew grimmer with every word. "I'm so sorry, Abbey."

"Oh! And let's not forget that word of our alleged engagement has already reached Crystal down at the diner, which I found out when I went to pick up our lunch order. Meaning basically everybody knows, and I couldn't even walk down the street to my car for people stopping me to offer congratulations and ask why it had been such a secret."

"What did you say?" There was a tension in his shoulders as he waited for her answer. Wondering whether she'd made the whole situation worse? Tried to tell the truth?

"The theme of the day was, 'No comment.' There was no sense in trying to correct Crystal in the moment. The explanation would've taken longer, and I didn't know who might be listening."

He seemed to relax at that. At the idea that there were fewer versions of the story to try to combat?

"That's probably best until we sort out how to handle this."

She didn't like it, but even she understood that the fewer people who knew, the better. But she couldn't fathom having to put this much thought into everything, all the time. "How the hell do you deal with this? With the invasion of your privacy? With people's entitlement, thinking they have any right to know about the intimate details of your life? After everything that happened around the trial, I never imagined you'd tolerate this at all."

He turned away and gave the red beans and rice a stir. "I don't love it, but it's part and parcel of the business. Although they tend to be a little more respectful of me directly. My publicist has coached me on how to handle the media. Not that she ever had something like this in mind."

"Well, you're going to have to do something about this. The insanity has to stop. I can't live like this, and it's sure as hell not fair to your sisters and the business we've built."

At the thump, thump, thump on the front porch, they both moved in that direction. Of course, Granddaddy wouldn't do as asked and stay put.

Kyle kept his voice low. "I've got some ideas about that we can discuss after Granddaddy goes to bed. Let's just get through dinner and after. I'll go put the tools away."

She could wait that long.

CHAPTER 6

$\mathcal{A}$s he waited for Abbey to get Granddaddy settled for the night, Kyle poked around the living room cabinets, hunting for the small-batch apple brandy they'd sometimes nipped from in high school. He figured they could both use something to take the edge off for this conversation.

The last thing he'd ever wanted to do was make her life harder. He'd known the press would follow up and be interested in her, but he'd underestimated how much and how fast they'd interfere. She'd looked so frazzled and tired when she got home. And it had only been a day. A part of him wondered if he should try to do as she'd asked and issue a retraction. He'd look like a fool at best, but in the grand scheme of things, what did that matter?

Still, a bigger part wanted to take this risk, make this pitch to her. It was a lunatic idea. Granddaddy's idea. One predicated on her not understanding the realities of his world or thinking too hard about it. The logic was less than sound, but he'd always loved a good Hail Mary. If she said no, that was it. This unexpected opportunity to make amends would disappear like so much smoke. He could always shoot for a retraction then. But for now, he had to try.

"He's finally down. You wore him out."

"I'm sorry. I tried not to let him overdo—"

"No, that wasn't a criticism. It's good. He'll sleep better this way." Abbey curled onto one end of the sofa.

Kyle crossed to her, offering a glass.

"Found the apple brandy. Figured you could use some after the day you had."

Gratitude flashed across her face as she took it. "Thanks." She closed her eyes as she sipped, savoring the flavor. The hint of a smile curved her lips as she dropped her head back. "I'll never forget that time we got caught filching some our junior year. Daddy was so mad, and you took all the heat, even though it was my idea."

Because her tone was fond, Kyle took the risk and eased onto the opposite end of the couch, rolling his own glass between his palms. "What was he gonna do to me? I'd had worse from my own parents almost every day growing up."

Her eyes cracked open, went serious. "You disappointed him. That was worse on you than if he'd raised a hand to you."

Uncomfortable with the truth of it, he twitched his shoulders and sipped. "I was surprised he didn't forbid you from hanging out with me."

"I was afraid he would, so I came clean after you left that night."

He stared at her. "You never told me that."

She shrugged, dropping her gaze and taking another drink. "I knew what our family was to you. I wasn't going to take that away."

There was something in her tone, some thrum of pain he didn't understand. But before he could follow up on it, she'd blanked her face again. "So, what are your ideas on how to fix this?"

Showtime.

"I think I know a way to make this go away. But you're not going to like it." With another sip for courage, he launched in. "You're gonna need some help with Granddaddy beyond a day or two. I can stay and do that. In the meantime, we maintain the engagement, do a few public appearances so that we can control the narrative of the media. We make them love us as an us, fall in love with you, and then you can publicly throw me over in whatever way you want so that the world knows we're over and it's my fault. It'll throw all the attention back on me as the bad guy, and you should be able to get back your peace and quiet."

Abbey stared at him. "You actually expect me to play along with this? Pretend to be in love with you in front of cameras and the world… my friends, my family, my *town?*"

The incredulity in her voice stung. "Once upon a time, you wouldn't have had to pretend."

The neutral mask cracked. "Don't you dare throw that in my face after what you did." The raw hurt in her eyes cut deep, and he didn't have the first clue how to apologize.

"Abbey, I'm sorry. I know it's too little, too late, and doesn't begin to make up for—"

"You're right, it doesn't. I'm not discussing that, Kyle."

He'd thought he understood, but seeing the pain in her face, fresh as if it happened yesterday, he knew this ran so much deeper than he'd ever suspected. And what he'd imagined had been untenable. Maybe he was fooling himself that she'd ever forgive him. Maybe he didn't deserve it.

"Okay. I want to be clear that the offer of help with Granddaddy has nothing to do with the rest of this. It's not contingent. Your family was always good to me, and I want to help."

There was that flash of... something again. He almost thought it was insult. But what sense did that make?

She looked away, her jaw working. "You think this is the only way to make this go away?"

Knowing it probably made him the worst kind of asshole, Kyle doubled down. "It's the best I've got without cluing my PR manager into the truth."

"And how long do you think this charade would need to go on?"

"I don't know. Until some fresh scandal or happening distracts them from us." *Until you soften enough to hear me.*

Abbey stayed quiet for several long moments. Then she tipped back her glass and drained the last of the apple brandy. "Fine. I'll do the dog and pony show. I'll play nice. And we get this over with as soon as possible."

Not exactly a ringing endorsement of his questionable plan, but it felt like getting a stay of execution. He'd have his chance. He sure as hell didn't plan to waste it.

"Okay. I'll touch base with Deanna—my publicist. See what she recommends."

"You're going to have to have a family meeting. Your sisters are perfectly well aware we haven't been talking for years, and I already told them the truth, so if you want to pull this off, they're all going to have to be on board."

Joy. He could imagine how well that was going to go over. Abbey wasn't the only one he'd left behind, and he'd have to reckon for that too. "Okay. Do they know about—"

"No. I wasn't eager to share that particular humiliation."

Shoving to her feet, she strode toward the stairs.

It wasn't because I didn't love you. I was a dumbass. The words log-jammed in his throat. She didn't want to hear any of that. She probably never would. But at some point, before all of this was over, he was going to say it, going to explain it, if for no other reason than hoping it dimmed some of the pain he'd caused her.

At the foot of the stairs she paused, without looking back. "Thank you for helping with Granddaddy."

Knowing there was nothing more for him to say, he kept his mouth shut, listening as she climbed to the second floor. For a long time after, he sat alone with his thoughts and his many, many regrets. Then he carried his guitar out to the front porch. The music had been calling him, as this place had been calling. At least if everything with Abbey went to hell, he'd have most of a new album.

As he began to pick out the melody in his brain, he wished that were more of a comfort.

~

"You're an eejit."

The flat pronouncement, delivered in Pru's husband's Irish brogue, was almost enough to make Abbey snort with laughter. It was so very obvious the rest of the family agreed with his assessment of the plan Kyle had laid out for them.

Kyle just crossed his arms and knit his brow, looking askance in Flynn's direction. "Didn't you and Pru have that whole fake engagement because of a social worker?"

"To be sure," Flynn conceded. "But we were already half in love with each other. I have grave concerns you'll be able to convince anyone of the truth of this."

A chorus of agreement rose up from the gathered siblings and their spouses. It was a fair concern. Abbey got prickly and angry every time anyone brought Kyle up in front of her. She shut down any conversations, as much out of fear that they'd keep prying to find out what really happened as because thinking of him simply hurt.

Kyle spread his hands. "If any of you have other ideas, I'd love to entertain them, but this is what we've got right now."

This was her opportunity to get out of this lunatic scheme. They had told no one else. There was still time to do something else.

"How about you fixing your own shit and leaving Abbey out of it?" Xander suggested. When Kennedy popped her husband's arm, he shrugged. "What? Somebody had to say it."

The protectiveness of her friends warmed something in Abbey's heart, even if they didn't know what they were protecting her from.

If the front united solidly on her side bothered Kyle, he didn't show it. "It's a fair question. If I thought a simple retraction would get the paparazzi off Abbey's back, I'd have done it already. But you'll find they're seldom interested in the truth. They only care about what sells."

"That's true enough," Athena agreed. As an award-winning chef with some notoriety, Kyle's youngest sister had faced her own battles with bad publicity. "So give them something more interesting. Go out with Mercy Lee."

His expression flattened, conciliatory attitude gone in a blink. "Absolutely not. I'm not going anywhere near that woman."

"Someone else then," Maggie suggested.

Kyle snorted. "Contrary to what you may think, I don't exactly have a digital Rolodex of the famous in my phone."

"Anything has to be better than you using Abbey," Pru insisted.

The warm fuzzies slid into discomfort. Angry as she was at Kyle, she didn't like seeing the people he counted as family—or had—piling on him like this. He needed them as a source of support, and it was as much her fault as his that he'd lost that.

"He's not using me if I agree to it. Which I did."

Abbey didn't miss the look of distress in Pru's eyes. "What do you get out of this?"

She'd thought about this a lot last night after she'd gone up to bed and begun second-guessing her decision. But his lunatic scheme gave her the chance at the one thing she hadn't had in a decade. "Closure."

None of them could argue with that. She'd been a walking case of unfinished business all these years, and they all knew it. Maybe she wouldn't have chosen this, and maybe she would've preferred to never lay eyes on him again, but she couldn't deny the appeal of finally, permanently resolving things.

Maggie's husband, Porter, a foster brother himself, broke the tense silence. "Even if you agree with this, I'm with Flynn. I don't see how anyone's going to believe it. You're a cactus any time he comes up. And you're supposed to act in love with each other in the public eye?"

Abbey swallowed. Because she'd thought of that, too. "I can sell it."

She just had to pretend they were still twenty-one. That the last several years hadn't happened. That Kyle was still the boy who'd dreamed with her under the stars, in a tree-house on the edge of her family's apple orchard.

That he hadn't left her at the altar.

Every face in the room showed skepticism and concern. Abbey ignored the clearly telegraphed "just because you can, doesn't mean you should" she was getting from Pru.

Closing her eyes for a moment, she brought back the boy in her mind, pulling up that memory of heady young love she'd shoved deep into mental mothballs and letting it flow through her. She felt her face and posture soften, and when she opened her eyes to look at Kyle, she saw the him he used to be. And letting the fantasy she'd clung to for years rule her—that he'd actually come when she'd suggested changing things between them—she rose to her toes and kissed him.

It was different coming to this with intent, with lifelong affection and a clear head. There was heat underneath. But it wasn't like the storm of a kiss from when he'd burst in on her at the spa. This was slow and sweet, full of all the years of yearning. He wrapped around her, and when he would have taken them deeper, she eased back. In his deep blue eyes she saw... or thought she saw... everything she'd wanted to see all those years ago. Which just proved he was a better actor than she'd thought.

"Well, that's... convincing."

She didn't know who'd spoken. Didn't care.

Yeah, she could sell the idea that she was in love with him because she wasn't having to act at all. Damn it. But he'd already broken her heart. How much worse could this be?

Feeling self-conscious, Abbey stepped back.

"Okay, maybe this is an obvious question,

but why didn't y'all ever get together for real?" Of course Pru's teenage daughter, Ari—the resident romantic—would ask that.

Abbey didn't at all want to talk about this, but she was legitimately curious what Kyle would say. Arching a brow, she punted the question to him.

"She was always way too good for me." He answered Ari, but his eyes stayed on Abbey. It was so very clear he stilled believed it. That he was still letting his parents and the damage they'd done to him run his life.

It infuriated and saddened her all over again. "You were the only one who thought that."

"No, I wasn't."

Temper ignited, as it often did when anything about his parents came up. "Oh, bullshit. After all these years, you're still letting their opinions dictate your behavior and your life. What is it going to take to get through that thick skull of yours? The *only* opinions that matter are those of the people who love you.

The *only* thing you're responsible for are *your* words and actions. You weren't the one tried and found guilty, so stop acting like it's on you to make reparations. It's not. It never was."

Kyle stared at her, throat working for several long moments. "It's been a long, long time since anybody's defended me to me. Nobody ever did it quite like you."

The idea that no one in his life would or could call him on this shit broke her heart. He had so thoroughly cut himself off from home and his past, other than a handful of his foster siblings, that he'd essentially cut himself off from support. From the people who would tell him what he needed to hear instead of what he wanted. Was it any wonder that the life he'd led had changed him?

With a sinking feeling, she realized she'd had a role in that. She'd excised him from her life. She'd had to for her own survival. But she was stronger now, and they were in this strange situation for however long it lasted.

She could do that for him again. Be that for him. Maybe he'd be the better for it.

With far more nonchalance than she felt, she fisted her hands on her hips. "Then you'd best clean your ears out. I've apparently got years of bullshit to call you on."

He actually grinned at that. "Can't wait."

"So, you're really going through with this?" Pru asked.

Kyle finally swung toward his family again. "Look, I know y'all are angry with me, and I've got a lot to make up for. That's justified. But I'd appreciate your support in this."

"We'd appreciate it," Abbey added, knowing they were following her lead.

His sisters exchanged serious looks with their spouses. In the end, Kennedy spoke for all of them. "All right. If that's really what you want."

Kyle sighed in relief. "Thank you. There's one more thing. I'll do what I can to steer the press away from the Ridge, but there are no guarantees. I don't want my local history brought up. I don't want people talking about my time with Joan because that will come back to my parents, and I've done everything possible to distance myself from them."

Of course he had. That had started well before he'd left Eden's Ridge. He was ashamed of his past and always had been. She needed to remember that and remember that this whole thing was just for show, no matter how he was acting now.

Porter crossed his arms. "I mean, sure, we'll respect that. But how are you going to control the rest of town?"

"I don't actually know, but I'm hoping if we direct the narrative, do some interviews in Nashville, it'll keep prying locally to a minimum."

"That's all well and good, but you have to sell it here, too," Ari pointed out. "Y'all gotta have a date night, at least. Give the gossips fodder to support the fiction you're presenting."

Kyle went brows up. "Should I be concerned that the teenager is this well-versed in how to deal with this kind of situation?"

"Please," Ari scoffed. "It's completely obvious. And this isn't my first rodeo."

"I mean, she's not wrong. We all know how the Ridge works. You give them half a story to run with, they'll fill in the rest," Kennedy said.

"And there are enough busybodies and romantics to take your well-known childhood friendship and build in a whole host of stuff that maybe didn't actually happen but fits with what you're presenting," Maggie added. "It'll make them feel good to say, 'Well, I knew it all along.' It could make them your best asset."

The idea of a fictional romantic version of her relationship with Kyle becoming part of Eden's Ridge collective memory made trepidation crawl up Abbey's spine. She'd have to live with that for the rest of her life when this was over. Was she prepared for that? It didn't actually matter either way now, did it?

"I take your point, but we can't leave Granddaddy alone for the sake of a public date night. We only managed to keep him occupied while we're here because of his poker game. For that matter, how the hell are we going to get loose to go to Nashville for interviews?"

"Oh, I've got you covered for that," Athena promised. "I'll bring him out to help film an episode of *The Misfit Kitchen* that's entirely about apples. We've been talking about it forever and just haven't gotten around to it since Logan and I adopted the boys. It'll be multi purpose: You and Kyle have time to do whatever needs doing. I get another episode in the queue. The orchard gets some additional publicity, and your granddaddy's sweet tooth is satisfied. It's a win all around."

Abbey wasn't sure she'd call a series of interviews a win for her, but she appreciated the gesture all the same.

"There are a bunch of us and just two of you. We can entertain your granddaddy so you can have a night off," Pru assured her. "Even without all of this going on, you took a lot on yourself to give your parents the gift of that cruise. You deserve a break."

It meant a lot to Abbey that, even though Pru was unabashedly worried about this whole setup, she was still willing to help. "Thanks."

CHAPTER 7

Kyle opened the farmhouse door to Griff. "Did you get it?"

"Yeah. Exactly where you said." His brother stepped inside and handed over the thing he'd been sent all the way back to Nashville to retrieve. His penetrating gaze was steady. "You wanna tell me why you had that just waiting around in your loft?"

"Not particularly." Hearing footsteps on the stairs, Kyle slid it into his pocket. "Thanks for picking it up. And thanks for helping out tonight with Granddaddy."

"There's a James Bond marathon running on TV. If two men can't bond over 007 and barbeque, there's something wrong with the world."

"Did you bring extra sauce and cobbler?" Granddaddy demanded from his position in the living room recliner.

"What do you take me for? A newb?" Griff held up the rest of his bags. "I even got ice cream for the cobbler."

"Good man," Granddaddy announced. "*From Russia with Love* is starting in ten minutes."

"Plates in the cabinet to the left of the sink."

At the sound of Abbey's voice, Kyle turned and promptly lost all train of thought.

The dress was turquoise, with full, lacy sleeves that dropped down to her wrists. A wide, brown leather belt cinched beneath her breasts and emphasized curves that were more pronounced than they'd been when she was a willow-thin teenager. Curves he wanted to get his hands on.

He'd waited for her down here countless times through the years. To go to school. To head into Johnson City for a movie. To hit up a football game. Or just to drive around town to see what there was to see. He'd seen her in cut-offs, overalls, jeans, and everything in between. He'd certainly seen her in a dress before—they'd double-dated for prom. But the effort had never been for him.

Okay, this probably wasn't for him either. It was part of the show they were putting on. And, hell, maybe she just enjoyed dressing up for herself. A lot of women did. But it didn't stop him from appreciating the way the boots put her right at the perfect height for kissing or how the pretty berry-stain gloss on her lips seemed to invite just that.

"Wow." Kyle had to pause and clear the gravel from his voice. "You look amazing." He hoped he wasn't drooling.

"Thanks."

Did he imagine her gaze darkening as they slid down his Wranglers and crisp, button-down shirt? Maybe. But he didn't think the extra color flaring in her cheeks was an illusion as she looked away again.

"Oooee, Butter Bean! You're a picture," Granddaddy declared.

She grinned and dropped a kiss to his leathery cheek. "I clean up pretty well. You two have fun. And don't eat too much dessert." With two fingers, she pointed at Griff and back at herself to indicate she'd be keeping an eye on them.

"You know that's an oxymoron, right?" Griff asked.

Abbey sighed. "At least eat dinner *first*."

He exchanged a grin with Granddaddy. "No promises."

Kyle wiped his clammy hands on the seat of his jeans. "You ready?"

She grabbed her purse. "Let's go."

"Have fun, kids!" Granddaddy sang.

Woman on a mission, as always, she beat

him out the front door. Kyle trailed her down the steps, lengthening his stride to get to the passenger side door of the Land Cruiser and open it for her. One golden brow lifted, but she slid inside without comment.

This whole situation was built one lie on top of another. But despite it all, Kyle was determined to do this right and take her on a real date. Growing up, he'd never pressed for anything more than friendship, not wanting to risk losing the easy way they were with each other. But it didn't mean he hadn't wanted more, hadn't imagined how he'd try to woo her. Maybe he'd never thought of doing it under these circumstances, but he was the first to understand that beggars couldn't be choosers, so he'd work with what he had. He wanted to remind her that they could have fun together. To hit on as much nostalgia as possible, since that seemed to soften her. God knew, he had a lot of work to do to make the closure she wanted wasn't him taking a permanent exit from her life.

A scrap of lyrics formed in his head as he climbed into the driver's seat. *First date, last chance.*

His fingers twitched against the steering wheel, mentally picking out the melody to go with the line.

"Need to write it down?"

Kyle glanced over to find Abbey's lips curved in faint amusement. "What?"

"I haven't forgotten that look. Write it down, so you won't lose it."

Appreciating the chance, and warmed by the fact that, on this at least, she still knew him, he slid out his phone. Opening the notes app where he dumped all his random ideas, he typed it in for posterity. Since he was going for nostalgia tonight anyway, he opened his music and navigated to a playlist of Abbey's favorites. Because, of course, he had one. He listened to it when he missed her. Which was... most of the time.

As the unmistakable rhythm of KT Tunstall's "Black Horse and the Cherry Tree" spilled out of the speakers, Abbey's faint smile turned into a full-on grin, and she was nodding in time to the music. "Nice."

He put the SUV in gear, and she began to sing. Her voice was quiet and pitch perfect. When they'd been young, she never sang, except with him. That she'd still trust him with that was a gift. It was instinct to add harmony, habit to drum the steering wheel. By the time they made to the end of the long drive, he could almost think that everything was normal. Almost.

But it wasn't normal. There was a gulf between them, and it had been years since they'd been okay. Somehow, he was going to woo her, despite all of that.

"You're nervous." Her tone was full of surprise.

Pausing his thumb tapping, he glanced over. "A little. I'm surprised you're not." He hadn't seen any of her usual tells. Not the chewing on the inside of her lip or the twisting of her purse strap or edge of her skirt.

Dropping her head back against the seat, she closed her eyes for a moment. "I'm too tired to be nervous."

It was an opening for a genuine conversation. Kyle jumped on it. "When was the last time you had the kind of break you're giving your parents?"

Her shoulders lifted in a shrug. "Before I moved home. Going on three years now, I guess."

"It's hard to do the go go go without a break. I get it. I mean, obviously not for the same reasons. But pushing like that, even doing something that matters, it burns you out. I haven't had a stretch off longer than a few days for about as long."

"Really?"

"Been on tour. One after another. Whatever time hasn't been on the road has mostly been in the studio. Rinse and repeat."

"That's not what I imagined you'd been doing."

Kyle could hear the bitter edge to his own laugh. "The reality of the music business isn't much like what I imagined when I started out." He could've gone on. Could have talked about the grueling schedules, the increasing lack of privacy, the politics of having to play nice with the label execs, even when they were patently wrong. But he didn't want to remind her of all the years they'd been apart or the reason for it, and they'd arrived at Elvira's Tavern.

There was live music tonight, which meant a crowd. That meant they'd be visible, which was the primary point of this whole outing. He hoped they could both reach a stage where that wasn't forefront in their minds tonight. Where they could just enjoy each other as they used to.

Abbey didn't wait for him to come around and open the door. She'd never been one to wait around for much of anything. But as they met at the front of the SUV, he took her hand. She jolted, just a little, before curving her fingers slowly around his. Warm and steady, her touch grounded him, that tangible link settling some of the nerves. At least until he tugged open the door.

The interior of the bar was crowded, with several clusters of patrons waiting to be seated. Abbey made eye contact with the hostess and held up two fingers. At the woman's nod, they moved themselves out of the way, into an empty corner. Kyle tucked Abbey close, as much because he wanted to as not to take up too much space.

She came willingly, sliding her arms around his waist, hooking her fingers in his back belt loops, and tipping her face up to his. The din of the crowd drowned out most conversations. Of course, that was why he dipped his head lower, close enough to catch a whiff of something floral she'd dabbed onto her throat. He resisted the urge to nuzzle for a better sniff.

"So what was different about the music business?"

Surprise distracted him from the feel of her in his arms. "I didn't think you'd want to know."

Her lips brushed his ear as she answered, and Kyle had to suppress a full-body shiver at the contact.

"I didn't let myself want to know. But as your fiancée, I'll be expected to."

Right. This was all part of the ruse. The easy affection. Finally asking him something about his life. She was a better actress than he gave her credit for. But, damn it, he wasn't going to get what he wanted if he kept reminding himself of the deception. So he'd treat all of this as the gospel truth until it either became true or she kicked him out of her life for good.

ABBEY WASN'T AT ALL sure she wanted to know about his career. But it was too easy being like this, all snugged up against him, with his arms wrapped comfortably around her, as what felt like everybody in town watched them. The part of her that was no longer fighting her feelings was desperate to believe the fiction they were weaving, and that was so very dangerous. She needed the reminder of why he'd left, what he'd been doing during all those years away from her. The reminder of the guy he was now, not who he'd been. And his fiancée *would* know this stuff. She needed to study up.

His familiar blue eyes—not hidden by the Clark Kent glasses tonight—searched hers for a long moment. "It's... exhausting. I knew there'd be touring. As an artist, you hope for that because it means the label believes enough in you to fund it. And I do love performing. But I thought there'd be more downtime between for just living. I was expecting a sort of work hard, play hard situation. The reality can be more of a slog. Which makes me sound ungrateful for my success. I'm not. But my wants take a backseat to the expectations of the label, and I'm burning out. Being on tour for the last six months with a woman I despise certainly didn't help that."

None of the old anger and resentment bubbled up at his words. He may have gotten what he wanted, but it came at a steep price. Abbey didn't see the spark she'd always associated with him. It was exactly what she'd been afraid of for him when he left. That it wouldn't be what he thought, and he'd lose himself. He'd wanted that, to a point. Wanted to distance himself from who he'd been in Eden's Ridge.

At twenty-one, she'd believed that he'd gone too far, become someone else. It was the only way she could reconcile what he'd done. But it wasn't a stranger who'd come back to the Ridge. Every hour in his company made that more and more clear. And that terrified Abbey as much as enticed her.

"Why Abbey Whittaker, as I live and breathe! I heard the rumors, and I just didn't believe it."

Abbey's fingers flexed in Kyle's belt loops as she braced herself to face the start of the onslaught. Once one broke the politeness barrier, more would follow, like sharks scenting blood in the water. This was the real deal. The moment they confirmed the rumors rather than ignoring them.

"Mrs. Lowrey, how good to see you." Kyle shifted Abbey to one side, so they presented a united front.

It was hard not to stare as he visibly turned *on*. Broad smile, open, friendly gaze. She'd heard the nickname forever ago—country music's Captain America, and she'd thought it idiotic. But in this moment, he was absolutely rocking the Steve-Rogers-nice-guy vibes.

Jolene Lowrey all but fanned her blushing cheeks. "You remember me?"

"Now, how could I possibly forget the maker of the best red velvet cake this side of the Mississippi?" He leaned a little toward her, lifting a hand to his mouth as if to impart a secret. "And best I've had on the other side, too."

"You charmer, you!" Her shrewd eyes shifted to Abbey, who instinctively stayed glued to her alleged fiancé's side. "I'd heard you two were engaged."

Multiple other people actively took a step closer, and Abbey had to resist trying to hide behind Kyle. This scrutiny was so much harder than she'd imagined.

Knowing she had a part to play, she tipped her head to his shoulder and hoped she looked besotted. "Yes, ma'am. There's nothing like marrying your best friend."

Mrs. Lowrey's expression softened. "After decades of being married to my own, I can certainly second that. Congratulations!"

"Thank you. I'm a lucky man."

"Well, let's see the ring!"

The ring. *Oh hell.* Neither of them had thought of that. People thought they were engaged. They expected a ring. It was part of the telling of the news to show it off.

Scrambling to cover, Abbey offered a regretful smile. "It's being sized, I'm afraid."

Kyle shifted. "Actually, I just got it back from the jeweler. Meant to give it to you before we left the house." Before she could ask what the hell he was up to, he reached into his pocket and pulled out a ring box, flipping it open with one hand, right there in the middle of the tavern's lobby.

The ring was simple and perfect, not the flashy or gaudy statement some people might've made in defense of a phony engagement. It was a real ring, and Abbey could only stare, speechless. There was no jeweler in town. He'd been here for days. With her or with Granddaddy. When did he have a chance to get this? And where?

As her brain spun, he plucked the ring from the box and took her hand. Abbey's heart thundered, some deep instinct of self-preservation urging her to *run run run run run*. God, she remembered waiting for this all those years ago. Nervous. Excited. So very in love because they'd finally both admitted they wanted to keep the pact they'd made as children.

But he hadn't come.

Abbey tried to hold on to the devastation of that as he looked into her eyes, but it dimmed as he slid the ring onto her left hand. His fingers were warm and sure, his eyes oh-so-serious as he settled the ring in place. The metal of the band was warm and felt made just for her.

While she struggled not to gape like a fish, he brought her hand to his lips, brushing a kiss over the knuckles. "Perfect fit."

It was an act. He'd waited to do this here, where they'd be seen and talked about. But it didn't feel like an act with his ring on her finger and his hand laced with hers. Not with his full attention on her, as if they were the only two people in the room. He seemed... sincere. He'd seemed sincere from the moment he walked back into her life. The part of her that still loved him, still so desperately missed her best friend, wanted to believe that this was real.

Oh, she was in so much trouble.

"Whittaker, party of two."

Abbey could've hugged the hostess for the interruption. She was too shaken to say a word, so it was Kyle who made their excuses to the assembled crowd and led her after the hostess with a hand on her lower back. They sat at a table in a corner. When she still couldn't seem to find her voice, Kyle ordered their drinks. Apparently, he still remembered the half-sweet, half-unsweet tea she preferred.

After the server walked away, he leaned in close, wrapping his hand around hers. "Abbey, say something."

She couldn't stop running her thumb along the underside of the band, feeling the unarguable proof that it was really there. "When did you pick this up?" Her voice sounded somehow far away. Maybe she was in shock. Surely, this qualified.

"Ten years, four months, sixteen days ago."

Abbey's gaze snapped to his. "But that would mean…"

"It's the actual ring I bought for you."

She shook her head, as much in confusion as denial.

If he'd bought a ring, then why hadn't he come? Why had he sent that horrible man in his stead?

For the first time, the need for that explanation was greater than the hurt. She wanted to ask, to demand the truth. She didn't dare do it here. Not with all these potential listeners. But it was the first time she'd allowed herself to wonder if there was more to the story than she'd believed all these years.

He brushed his thumb down her ring finger, lighting little fires along the way. "I wanted you to know it was yours. I didn't mean to bring up something painful. Let's just have fun tonight, okay?"

Fun? They were supposed to have *fun*, when everything she'd believed about him for ten years might be wrong?

The band set up on the little stage began to play, saving her from the burden of conversation. But it didn't save her from wondering whether she'd misjudged him.

They ordered food. She had no idea what she'd asked for and didn't much care. The band was good. Country and southern rock covers bouncing around the past couple of decades. Kyle kept her entertained with random music trivia and jokes, and Abbey gradually relaxed, forgetting about the ring for whole minutes at a time. Maybe she actually could pull off this whole looking like a happily engaged woman thing.

As the band rolled into a slow song, Kyle shoved back in his chair and held out a hand. "C'mon."

Abbey blinked at him. "What?"

"You love this song. Let's dance."

She did love this song. "Old Love Feels

New" was one of her favorites by Chris Young because it so reminded her of the story Granddaddy told about how he met Grandma Ruth. But… "No one's dancing."

"So we'll be the first." He wiggled his fingers. "Dance with me, Abbey."

After a long, long moment, she took his hand and let him pull her out to the little empty space in front of the corner where the band was set up. She hadn't danced with him since prom, and even then, it was just for fun, while her date tried to salvage his tux from an incident with the punch. He hadn't held her like this, close enough to feel the heat of his body and the rasp of his jeans against her legs as they moved to the beat of the music. After all the years of nothing but easy friendship, and then the years of distance, being in his arms like this was… unnerving.

She could feel everybody's eyes on them, but kept hers on his in defense. All Kyle's focus stayed on her, as if he didn't notice everyone staring. He'd been a pretty decent dancer back when. He was better now. It felt way too good to be held by him, way too tempting to let go and fully immerse herself into this fiction.

Soulmates. The song was about soulmates. She'd once believed he was hers. As she swayed with him, listening to his easy baritone singing just loud enough for her to hear, with so much seeming honesty in his eyes, she wanted to believe it again. Her heart beat thick in her throat, and she found herself edging closer, lifting her face to his as he lowered his head.

The smattering of applause had them both pausing, their mouths a breath apart. The song was over, and so was the moment. Reluctance in every line of his body, Kyle let her go. "Looks like our food arrived."

They walked back to their table, and she soaked in the bittersweetness of being close to him again, understanding that this whole charade would break her so much worse the second time around.

CHAPTER 8

"I feel sick." Abbey's cheeks were pale beneath the blush the makeup technician had added, and her hands were knit together in her lap.

Kyle felt awful about it. How could it not have occurred to him that she'd be absolutely terrified of a TV interview? She'd always hated public speaking.

Deanna James, his publicist, beamed an encouraging smile at Abbey. "You'll do fine. You're gorgeous, and you snagged one of country music's hottest bachelors. You're the one going home with him. So, just remember that if you start to think about the other women watching and wishing they were you."

He wasn't sure that would do a damned thing to help, even if their situation was exactly what it appeared to be from the outside. Moving closer, he squeezed Abbey's shoulder and found her stiff as a board. "It's just a conversation, Abs. Pull out your best talk-to-a-stranger-at-the-church-pot-luck skills." She could talk to literally anyone if it wasn't in a formal setting.

Abbey glared at him. "There are no lights or cameras at a church potluck."

"Would it help if I asked craft services for some of those off-brand sandwich cookies?"

"I couldn't keep them down even if they had them."

Oh, this was bad. But he just hadn't realized. She'd been so matter-of-fact about the entire process once Deanna told them they'd be having their public debut on True Country Network's *Countrified.* They'd spent the whole drive to Nashville in deep discussion about their story, getting on the same page and filling in some gaps in their knowledge about each other from the past decade. And that was on top of the two days of prep Deanna had put them through before they left Eden's Ridge, to make sure they were as ready as they could be.

Needing to find something to put her at ease before they went out on that stage, he reached way into their past. "Okay, then remember that nothing can be as bad as broccoli."

Deanna's blonde brow winged up. "Broccoli?"

Abbey sighed, the grim set to her mouth easing a little as she explained. "Our second-grade play was on the food groups. I was broccoli. Except I forgot my line, so Kyle raced onto the stage in his cheese costume, loudly insisting that broccoli wasn't a solo vegetable.

That she and cheese were better together. Delicious and nutritious. Nobody remembered I hadn't said a word."

"Awww." Deanna pressed a hand to her heart. "That is both adorable and hilarious. You two really have known each other a long time."

"Practically since diapers." Kyle knelt in front of the chair and took Abbey's sweaty hands in his. "I'll be right there with you. Anything goes wrong, I'll be the cheese again, okay?"

Her trembling hands tightened on his. "Promise?"

It did something to his chest to have her look at him with trust in those big doe eyes. He'd never thought she'd look at him like this again. And maybe it was only because this was his world, and he was the one who understood how to navigate it, but it didn't mean any less to him to have the chance. "Cross my heart."

She bit her lip, and Kyle wanted to kiss it better. "At least they won't ask me to sing."

Deanna's face twisted in sympathy. "Can't sing?"

"She sings beautifully."

"In the shower and the car. Not in front of *people*. I can't even sing louder than a whisper in the congregation at church on Sunday without feeling like I'm going to pass out."

So that hadn't changed in the last decade. And why should it? As bold and open as she was, she'd never longed for the limelight, never had the yen to perform. He was lucky she'd agreed to this much.

He thought about their drive into Eden's Ridge for their date the other night. "You sing with me all the time."

"You aren't people and car karaoke doesn't count."

Once upon a time it had been a lot more than car karaoke. They'd written songs together. But that had been a long, long time ago.

A tech approached, equipment in hand. "Okay, you two, let's fit you with mic packs."

Abbey kept hold of one of his hands. She'd softened some since the ring. They still hadn't talked about it. Their days had been full of Granddaddy and interview prep and work, and he hadn't wanted to rock the tenuous truce. But he'd caught her rubbing her thumb over the band, as she was now. Wondering? He hoped so. He intended to respect her pacing on this insofar as possible, let her ask in her own time for the truth she hadn't been willing to hear before.

As they waited in the wings to go on, he kept an arm around her, hoping she'd find the contact soothing. There was no room for nerves about selling a fake engagement to the public at large. All his focus was on making sure she was as comfortable as she could be.

Unlike *The Breakfast Club, Countrified* wasn't live, which Kyle preferred. But pre-filmed came with its own challenges—like the studio audience, which he knew would be worse for Abbey. At the signal, he took her hand and led her out beneath the lights, waving to the cheering crowd.

They shook hands with the host, Zac Muriel, and took their seats, side-by-side on the sofa.

"Well, we're delighted to meet you, Abbey. All of country music's fandom is terribly curious about you. Kyle's kept you a closely guarded secret for so long."

Her hand shook in his, but she managed a smile. "He knows I prefer it that way. I'm a small-town girl, who likes a quiet life."

"Fair enough." Zac smiled. "We appreciate you stopping by today to satisfy some of our curiosity. So, how did you and Kyle meet?"

"We grew up together. I literally don't remember a time when I didn't know Kyle. He's in all of my earliest memories. We were best friends since forever."

"And how did he propose?"

She angled her head and laughed. "Which time?"

Host blinked in surprise, shooting a glance in Kyle's direction. "You asked more than once?"

"The first time, we were six. She was my best friend, so it made all the sense in the world to me that we should get married. I took my entire allowance up to the grocery store in town and had it converted into change. They had one of those little candy and prize machines there, where you put in a quarter and got something in a little plastic bubble. I blew through almost all of it before I got one with a ring inside. And I asked her in the apple orchard where we played, after we hung upside down from one of the trees, to see who could stand having all the blood rush into their head."

Zac laughed. "Who won?"

"Oh, me," Abbey said. "I always won at that."

"I figured picking something you always won would butter you up."

Startled, she looked up at him, apparently forgetting her nerves. "Really? You never told me you did that on purpose."

"Besides offering the sage advice that you should marry your best friend, your grand-daddy also told me that the key to a happy life was a happy wife. You *loved* beating me at anything, so it seemed a good beginning."

Everybody laughed, including Abbey. "You didn't actually *ask*. You just said we were best friends and we should get married."

"*You* said we were too young, so I suggested twenty-one, which felt absolutely ancient at the time."

"And I said yes."

She had. And it had been the best day ever.

Zac seemed absolutely delighted. "That is adorable. So was this a childhood sweethearts kind of situation?"

"Not exactly. We were never actually romantically involved growing up." Abbey glanced at him. "That came later."

"So what about the second proposal? The grown-up one?"

Kyle had thought about this, about how he'd wanted to do it if he ever got the chance. "I took her back to the orchard. Back to that tree. Strung the whole thing up with fairy lights and brought her out for a picnic dinner after sunset. I learned a thing or three in the intervening years, but I had it right the first time. Because I knew I wanted to spend the rest of my life with my best friend."

Abbey's eyes were soft as they looked into his.

"Wow. So you decided to honor that marriage pact, even ten years after the deadline. Why the delay? Why not do it when you were twenty-one?"

I love you, Kyle. I've always loved you. And I think you've always loved me. What if we did this for real? What if we got married?

He could still remember the phone call that had changed everything for him.

And he remembered everything that came after.

"The planets just didn't quite align." It was as honest an answer as he could manage.

"Did it have anything to do with your parents being in prison?"

Kyle froze, though every muscle in his body wanted to leap across the desk and grab Zac by the lapels, demanding to know how he'd found out. Sweat broke out down his back. How? He'd done everything he could to distance himself, to keep this secret from his past.

Abbey's hand squeezed his almost hard enough to rub bone together, pulling his attention from the panic and the rage. He stared into her eyes, seeing the calm assurance she'd offered countless times in the past. *I've got you.*

Smoothly, she slid into the silence. "The gap in our relationship had nothing to do with anyone but us. We both had some growing up to do, dreams we wanted to follow." She looked back at him, warmth in her expression.

"But love finds a way to pull the right people back together at the right time."

This woman had always been his staunchest defender. He wanted so desperately for her words to be the absolute truth. To have her at his back forever.

Grateful beyond measure to have her as his, at least for this moment, Kyle lifted her hand and pressed a kiss to the back of it. "I'm an incredibly lucky man to have her support."

"Always." Abbey sent a radiant smile toward the host. "We're looking forward to setting a date for the wedding, now that he's done with the tour."

Kyle held his breath, waiting for Zac to press. But Abbey's redirect worked. He didn't pursue the line of questioning about Kyle's parents.

It took everything he had to hold on to his Nice Guy persona because he realized about halfway through the remainder of the inter-view how this information likely got leaked, and he sure as hell needed to make some discrete inquiries before he took legal action about it. So, it was Abbey who finished out the interview, fielding questions like a pro, being broccoli to his cheese as temper and questions continued to bubble and stew beneath the surface. Abbey who charmed the host and the audience. And it was Abbey who pulled him to his feet and kept him grounded as they waved farewell and walked off the stage.

When he would have stormed immediately out, she pulled him close, pressing her mouth to his ear. "This isn't my world, but even I know you can't lose it here. Hang onto whatever this is until we can get somewhere private."

Sucking in a long, slow breath, he nodded, wrapping his arms around her and burying his face in her hair until he thought he could face the rest of their obligations.

ABBEY STAYED quiet as Kyle unlocked the door to his loft. He'd been barely holding it together since the interview. She didn't dare push him to talk yet because she knew how carefully he'd guarded the truth about his parents. That they were in prison was only the tip of the iceberg. If that detail had gotten out, how much longer before the rest came to light?

Stepping inside behind him, she drank in the space, noting all the gorgeous, exposed brick in the huge, open loft. There was a modern, industrial rustic kitchen tucked along one wall. A big, cushy couch was arranged near wide windows that framed Nashville's skyline. She noted instruments—an upright piano and a few guitars, among which she recognized the battered Yamaha she'd bought him from the pawnshop when they'd been twelve. His first. Beyond the grouping of living room furniture, she saw a massive, king-sized bed with a slate-gray duvet. Only one corner of the loft had walls, presumably housing the bathroom.

Kyle shut the door and paced restlessly across the wide-planked floors. "It had to be him. He's the one with the knowledge and the contacts."

Evidently, he was finally ready to talk.

"Who?"

"Davis Lipscomb.

Abbey recognized the name and tensed. "Your manager?"

He seemed surprised she remembered that. "Yeah. Former. I fired him after *The Breakfast Club* interview because he was the one who went explicitly against my wishes and fed the host that bullshit about me being involved with Mercy Lee. It was the last straw."

There was vague satisfaction at that. She'd hated Lipscomb for years, despising his influence over Kyle. "Well, I'd say that was good riddance. He was useful for doing your dirty work, but I don't think much else."

Kyle stopped his pacing, a crease forming between his brows. "Dirty work? What are you talking about?"

She couldn't help scoffing. "You don't consider sending him in your stead to meet me dirty work?"

The absolute stunned shock on his face had her heart starting to pound. "What? When? I never sent him to you."

"What do you mean, when? When else, Kyle? He showed up at the chapel that day. Said you'd sent him to break the news that we wouldn't be getting married. He had a letter from you to prove it." A letter she'd read over and over, hoping to find some other explanation than the one in its lines.

Kyle was shaking his head, a muscle jumping in his jaw. "I never wrote anything. What did it say?"

Abbey's stomach began to knot, and she crossed both arms over her middle. "That you'd wrestled with it all night, and you realized you could never go through with it. A marriage would be too hard to maintain with the pressures of the road and staying single was better for your career."

Angry color flushed his face. "All arguments Davis threw at me when he tried to talk me out of it." Eyes narrowed, he studied her, seeing too much, as always. "There's something else. What more did it say?"

Abbey closed her eyes, feeling tears well up at the memory of the painful words she was now deathly afraid weren't even truth.

Kyle's footsteps drew closer. He cupped her cheek, his voice soft and urgent. "Abbey, what else did it say?"

She swallowed and opened her eyes, wanting to see his face as she told him this part. "That you were already handicapped enough by the secret of your parents, and you couldn't afford the burden of maintaining connections with anyone from Eden's Ridge. You needed a fresh start, and we weren't truly your family, anyway."

With every word, the blood drained out of his cheeks. "I didn't write that. I didn't send that. I would never. Your family... I would never in a thousand years besmirch your fam-

ily. They did so much for me. I'm not—I didn't
—Oh fucking hell... all these years you've
thought... No wonder you hate me."

She didn't. Hadn't, though she'd tried.

He took her hands, and Abbey felt him
shaking. "I didn't know. I swear to God, I
didn't know. I was coming to meet you. I told
him as much. He hated you. Thought you
were distracting me from my career. He was
furious I chose you. But he said, fine if I was
going to tank everything I was building, we
might as well have a drink first. The next
thing I knew, it was two days later, and I'd
missed our meetup. When I tried to contact
you, you wouldn't talk to me. For weeks,
months after. But I never... I... Abbey. Fuck, I
should have tried harder. I should have done...
something."

It hadn't been Kyle. All these years, her
memories of him had been tainted by this lie.
He hadn't betrayed her, hadn't rejected her
family. Her brain was spinning, rewriting history so fast she was all but dizzy with it. She

had so many questions, but she could only zero in on the most salient point. "You were coming? You chose me?"

His hands tightened on hers. "Yes. God, yes. I wanted everything you were offering because I was in love with you, too."

The tears overflowed. He wasn't the man she'd believed he was. He hadn't changed, hadn't thrown away a lifetime of friendship and the chance for more. She'd done that herself because she'd been ruled by hurt and stubbornness. All this time they'd lost because she hadn't trusted the voice deep down that knew him, knew he'd never have said those things.

"I thought… I thought… Oh, God. Kyle, I'm so sorry. I should have given you the chance to explain. After everything we'd been through, I owed you the chance to do that, and instead I…" A hiccupping sob tore free. "I broke us." And now… now he'd said "was." He *was* in love with her. Past tense.

"No." Kyle framed her face, his own twisted with pain. "No, baby, you didn't."

"But the things I believed of you. The way I cut you so completely out of my life. You should hate me."

"I could never hate you. You were hurt and misled, and I was so ashamed of my own mistakes, I didn't fight for you the way I should have."

Neither of them had fought the way they should have. "I don't blame you for giving up on me."

"I didn't." He dug into his pocket, held something out.

She stared at his palm, at the plastic ring she'd sent back to him a decade ago. "You kept it?"

"I carry it everywhere. It was the only piece of you I had left." He brushed gently at the tears still streaming down her cheeks. "Abbey, I've been in love with you all my life. And I know I don't deserve it but, God, if you could find it in you to give me another chance—to give *us* another chance—I won't let you regret it."

This was the answer her heart needed. With it, the shadow that had stretched over a third of her life vanished in a blaze of joy. There were so many more things to talk about, details to clear up, but none of that mattered in this moment. She had the truth, and no more reason to hold back.

CHAPTER 9

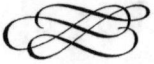

*A*t long last, the truth had come to light, and it was so much worse than Kyle had known. Him not showing up was bad enough, but Abbey thinking he'd actively thrown away her friendship, her family—almost nothing could have hurt her more.

She believed him. There was no question of that, not with the tears and instant self-recrimination. God, he hated that. Hated that she'd blame herself for believing someone else's lie. He'd needed to comfort and soothe. And he'd needed to ask for a second chance, even if she needed time to consider, to work through the views she'd held on to for so long.

But that wasn't his Abbey. She made swift, definitive decisions based on the information in front of her. Right now, that was him—humbled, desperate, and aching.

She launched herself at him, her arms wrapping around him, her lips colliding with his. Kyle staggered a step before he caught them both, hauling her closer and meeting her fevered kiss with his own as relief pulsed through him. There was no hesitation, none of the trepidation they'd both felt in the past about whether changing things was the right move. They'd both lived with years of regret. Now was the time to seize the moment they'd been given.

Spearing his hands into the silk of her hair, he slanted his mouth to take the kiss deeper. Tasting the salt of her tears, he vowed never to give her reason to shed them again. He'd do anything, everything, to make himself worthy of this woman.

Her hands tugged at the tails of his shirt, tunneling beneath the layers to skate over the muscles of his back. He shuddered at the touch, wondering how he'd survived all these years without knowing the feel of her hands on him.

Abruptly, she tugged away.

Kyle's heart plummeted. She'd changed her mind. Come to her senses.

But Abbey didn't let him go. Instead, she took his hand and towed him across the room, toward the bed.

He wanted her more than his next breath, but he hesitated, needing her to be sure. Dragging his feet, he tugged her to him. "Abbey. Slow down. We don't have to—"

Eyes molten, she lifted her chin in challenge. "Do you want me?"

"Yes." The word tripped off his tongue without hesitation. He'd always wanted her.

"Then please..." She rose to her toes, her lips a whisper away from his. "Don't make me wait."

Seeing the certainty shining in her eyes, he reached for the buttons on her shirt. Her hands lifted to do the same. They knew each other so very well, but this was uncharted territory for them both. They undressed each other, a dance of fast movements and long pauses to touch and taste each inch of newly exposed skin. Every moment was a gift he wanted to savor.

When she stood in her bra and panties, he urged her back, following her down onto the bed. She arched up as he covered her, as if she couldn't get enough skin-to-skin. He certainly couldn't.

"Let me," he murmured, kissing his way down her torso, nuzzling the valley between her breasts, stroking his hands along the flare of her hips.

He lingered over the scar on her thigh from a fall crossing a barbed wire fence when she was thirteen and the thin line along her collarbone from trying to make friends with their surly old barn cat when they were eight.

Physical signs of the history they shared. But he'd never seen them like this.

"Kyle." His name was a plea as she moved restlessly beneath him.

Shifting, he reached beneath her to open the clasp of her bra, drawing it away to free her breasts. A rosy flush bloomed on her chest as he stared. "So beautiful." They filled his hands, warm and firm and perfect. He bent to take one budded nipple into his mouth, loving the way Abbey gasped at the contact, threading her fingers in the hair at his nape to hold him in place. As her hips began to circle, he moved again, pressing a knee to her heated center. On a grateful moan, she began to move, seeking her release as he worshiped her breasts with his lips and hands.

The drawn-out cry of his name as she crested was the sweetest music.

Kyle kissed her again, long and slow, easing her down from the peak. She'd barely stopped shuddering before she reached for his jeans, yanking down his fly and reaching in to close her hand around the pulsing length of him.

He swore, part bliss, part frustration. Then they were both lost in a storm of frantic touching and tasting, rolling, grasping, gasping, until they were naked, and he had her pinned again, his crown just nudging at her entrance.

"Now," she begged, arching her hips to take the tip of him inside her.

Kyle froze. "Condom."

Abbey lost some of the dazed expression but none of the desperation. "Please tell me you have one."

"I... somewhere. Hang on."

Scrambling off the bed, he raced for the bathroom.

"Don't you have some in the bedside table?"

"I've never brought a woman here." Let her make of that what she would.

Yanking out drawers, he dug through toiletries until he located an unopened box. *If there is a God, these won't be expired.*

He checked the date and breathed out. "Hallelujah."

Fumbling the box open, he pulled out a packet, ripped it open, rolling it on as he hurried back to her.

Entirely unselfconscious, she sprawled on the mussed blankets, her hair spread out in a halo of gold, her body flushed and waiting like his most prurient fantasy. Kyle forced himself to slow as he came back to her. He wanted to memorize this moment and all the moments after as he stretched out over her, settling in the cradle of her hips. She reached between them, guiding him back to her entrance.

Kyle fixed his gaze on hers as he slipped inside her in one long, slow slide. Joy radiated in her smile, in the hitch and release of their synchronized breaths. All the desperation faded and time slowed down. Everything took on the honeyed hue of perfection because this feeling, with her, was what he'd been searching for his whole life. This was home. She was home.

"Abbey."

Bending, he captured her sigh as he began to move, losing himself to pleasure and the glide of skin on skin, in the heat they made together, until she quickened around him, and they both fell over the edge of delicious madness.

IN A HAZE OF POST-ORGASMIC BLISS, Abbey lay wrapped around Kyle, heart thudding, breath beginning to slow as she stroked her fingers through the soft hair at his nape. He'd collapsed on her, taking just enough weight on his elbows to keep from crushing her. She could still feel him twitching inside her as her body fluttered with aftershocks.

She'd just made love with her best friend. Former best friend? She didn't quite know what they were now. More. For the moment, that was all she needed.

He turned his face to kiss the side of her throat. She tipped her head back to give him better access, humming in pleasure and stroking a foot along his calf. How long it would take to rouse him enough for a second round?

"Be right back."

He pulled away, and she felt bereft at the loss of his heat. But the view of his naked ass as he strode into the bathroom couldn't be beat. She'd seen it once, back in high school, when he'd stripped down after a sweaty day of work to cool down in the pond on the farm. That glimpse of well-toned backside had in-spired a number of fantasies over the years. The adult reality was so much better.

On a sigh, she collapsed back against the pillows, feeling loose and used and deli-ciously relaxed for the first time in... she had no idea how long. Her mind lazily circled back around to what he'd said about never bringing a woman here. She wasn't under any delusion that they'd waited for each other, but she liked the idea that no one else had been in his bed, his private space. The last several days had given her a much clearer understanding of how important that privacy was to him. There was a very clear line between Public Kyle and Real Kyle. How often did he get to be really himself anymore?

The bed dipped as he came back, sliding in next to her and pulling her against his body. Abbey went willingly, snuggling in as he flipped the blankets over them both. The stroke of his hand along her back made her melt a little more into him, and she struggled against the pull of sleep. How delicious it would be to just give in until tomorrow? That wasn't on the table. There were responsibilities waiting back in the Ridge. But she wasn't going to think about that just yet.

"You okay?" His voice was a rumble against her ear.

"Mmm. I'm happy. And I'm sad. We lost so much time."

He brushed a feather soft kiss against her temple. "No more of that. We aren't wasting any more time on regrets. We're here now. It's just as you said—love brought us back together at the right time."

She couldn't stop herself from snorting. "I don't know if it was love so much as your big mouth. This whole cockamamie plan to get the press off our backs isn't going to work, is it?"

Unperturbed, he shrugged. "Probably not. But you were talking to me, and I was desperate not to lose that. Can't argue with the results."

Abbey sobered, struggling not to descend into regrets again. The questions she'd pushed off came flooding back. Better to ask them here, now, when they were certainly alone than to save them for later. "What really happened that day?"

He sighed. "I was packed and walking out the door when Davis found me. He'd booked another gig. I told him I couldn't do it, that I already had plans. He wouldn't let me just leave it at that, so I told him I was on my way to meet you. That we were eloping. Back then, he tried to maintain this kind of avuncular, I-know-best kind of attitude. He tried to talk me out of it, but when I didn't listen, he got more forceful, insisting that a marriage then would stall out all the momentum I'd built and ruin my career. I was on the cusp, and I couldn't afford to take my eye off the prize. I didn't care. What good was any of it without you? So he said, fine, we'd have one drink before I left. I figured that was the least I could do."

"You said the next thing you knew it was two days later. Was it really one drink?"

"I only remember one. It was weird. I've never been one to drink until I was blackout drunk. I remember toasting to our happiness and then...nothing."

Abbey could think of only one way that made any sense. "What if he drugged you?"

The hand he stroked along her skin went still. "What?"

She pushed up on one elbow so she could look into his face. "What if you were roofied? He didn't want you coming to me, and then he came himself with a letter he forged, ensuring I wouldn't be open to talking to you. Take me out of the equation and nothing distracted you from doing whatever it is he thought you should do. I don't imagine I'm wrong in thinking he's made a significant amount of money off you over the years."

Kyle arched a brow, considering. "I mean...yeah. Regardless of what kind of man he is, he is largely responsible for my career."

"No." Abbey shook her head and laid a hand over his heart. "You built your career. Your music. Your talent. No amount of marketing or connections can change that. He'd have had nothing without you, and he knew it."

"He pushed me to do a lot of things I wasn't exactly comfortable with. Nothing illegal, just taking some chances, getting outside my comfort zone. And it worked. But if he went so far as to drug me and lie to you, manipulate us both...what else did he do in the name of advancing his investment?" Obviously the idea didn't sit easy with him.

"It's something to look into. Will you confront him about today? Is there anyone else who could have leaked something about your parents?"

He hesitated before lifting his gaze to hers. "My mother is out of prison."

Abbey jack-knifed up on a gasp. "What?" She should have had more time left on her sentence.

"She showed up after my last concert." He said it calmly, but she knew it would have rocked him.

"Could she be responsible?"

"She doesn't have the connections. And if she'd told the story, it wouldn't have stopped with one question trying to get a rise out of me. She'd have told everything. Or her version of everything."

It was a reasonable assumption. But how long before she came back again, pressed him for… something?

"What did she want?"

He shook his head. "I don't know. I had Davis deal with her."

And this was probably part of what had ensured Kyle's loyalty to the man for years. He'd taken the burden of that ugliness off Kyle's shoulders so he could focus on his music. But with Davis fired, there was no one standing in front of him now. He'd have to deal with it sooner or later.

"She's not likely to stop trying to contact you." Twyla knew who he'd become. She'd want something. Restitution. Payback. Just to screw with him. "What will you—"

He cut her off. "I'll figure it out later. Right now, we need to get cleaned up and get on back to pick up Granddaddy."

Understanding the topic was closed for the moment, Abbey reached out to cup Kyle's cheek, bringing her lips to his in a gentle kiss. "I won't let you face her alone. Whatever's coming, were in this together."

He pressed his brow to hers, holding her close. "Thank you. Everything's better when I've got you by my side."

CHAPTER 10

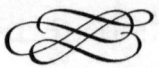

The house was quiet. Granddaddy had been so hyped up with excitement about his day on Athena's *Misfit Kitchen*, it had taken a while to get him to bed. Abbey had gone up to get ready for bed herself. Kyle wished he could join her, but he was too wound up to sleep, and no matter what had happened between them in his loft today, it didn't seem right to share her bed in this house. Not yet, anyway. They were still at the start of this... thing between them. And even though her folks were out of town, he couldn't stop imagining her father shooting off a glare of disapproval.

Hell, for all he knew, Abbey's father was sending one from the Caribbean. Or maybe not. Out to sea or not, if they'd seen the news of the engagement, he felt certain they'd have managed a phone call or an email demanding to know what was going on. Kyle no longer knew the answer to that question. This had started off as a fake engagement. But that was before they'd cleared the air, gotten on the same page. Fallen into his bed. They were unquestionably together, at last. But that on its own wasn't enough to make this engagement real. So he had no idea what they were going to tell her parents when they got home. Or exactly what they'd tell his own family, for that matter.

He wished that was the only thing he had to worry about. He wished he could just focus on the joy and relief of finally getting a true chance with her after all these years. But bound up in that joy was blistering fury at

Davis for the role he'd played in keeping them apart. If not for that interference, Abbey would be his wife. They might have started a family by now. They'd certainly have built a life together. Despite all his advice to her earlier that they should let go of the past and focus on the now, he felt the weight of every single one of those missed years with her.

Unable to sit still and needing to vent all this rage, Kyle strode outside, phone in hand. It was late, and Davis probably wouldn't answer anyway, but he had to at least *say* something, even if it was just a threat of legal action via voicemail.

But his former manager answered after only a single ring. "Kyle." He recognized the smooth, negotiator tone. "Well, I have to say, you lasted longer than I thought you would. I knew you'd see you couldn't do without me."

The unfathomable nerve of this man. "That's not why I'm calling."

"Oh?" There was an edge to the faint tone

of interest, the only thing that let Kyle know he was really listening.

"Why did you do it?"

"Why did I do what?"

"Why did you lie to her? To me?" The reason didn't really matter, but he needed to know.

"To who?"

Kyle's hand fisted around the phone. "You know damned well who. To Abbey. You had no right to interfere."

Davis dropped the congenial, I'm-completely-innocent tone. "I had every right to protect my investment in you. If you'd married her, you never would have made anything of yourself. You'd have run back home and wasted yourself on some small-town job because you couldn't bear to be away from her. You'd have none of the money, none of the acclaim, none of the career you've had."

"You can't know that. She would have supported me."

"Would she? Or would all the sacrifices

your career demanded have been too much? I did you both a kindness cutting that foolishness off before it ruined you."

Outrage boiled up, hot and deadly, driving him into a furious stride across the darkened yard. He needed to move, needed to hit something, needed some kind of outlet for all this frustration.

This man had run his life for years. Kyle had let him, believing Davis was looking out for his best interests. But the only interests Davis was protecting were his own. He'd been using Kyle for his own ends from the beginning, and abruptly, Kyle needed to know exactly how else he'd been manipulated. "What else did you do in the name of protecting your investment?"

"What I had to. You wouldn't have this career if not for me."

"And is that why you leaked the information about my parents? To prove you giveth and you can take away?"

"You're talking about that little stunt on *Countrified?* That wasn't me."

"Really. You expect me to believe that?"

"As you pointed out, I signed an NDA."

"No one else has reason to—"

"Listen to what's coming out of your mouth. Someone else very definitely has reason, and you ignored her. The way you've been ignoring them both for years. You want to blame somebody, look at your dear old mama."

The idea of that made Kyle's blood run cold. He wanted nothing to do with either of his parents. And he couldn't see his mother being behind this. "She wouldn't have stopped with just that piece. She'd tell everything."

"I'm inclined to agree with you. Not that it matters."

"If not either of you, then who?"

"Did it ever occur to you that you brought this on yourself? You're the one who told the world about Abbey. How long do you think it'll take a determined reporter to dig up the rest of your past? Much of it is a matter of public record if someone figures out where to look."

He wasn't wrong. There was only so much that could be protected by a legally changed name.

When he said nothing, Davis continued. "You can think what you want of me, but I wasn't wrong. You can never keep your past a secret if you don't cut yourself off from it. At this point, it's only a matter of time. I hope she's worth it."

"She's worth everything."

But his only answer was the weighted silence of dead air. Davis had hung up on him.

A sense of impending dread settled over him as he shoved the phone in his pocket. Today's interview would only be the first volley. More would follow, and what would be left of his reputation when it did?

Kyle realized he'd paced the hundred yards or so from the main house to the house where he'd lived with his parents. After they'd gone to prison, the Whittakers hadn't taken on more permanent help, so the house had been turned into lodging for seasonal employees. It had been painted, furniture changed out, landscaping updated. All that had happened before he'd left Eden's Ridge. But no amount of cosmetic change kept him from seeing what it had been for him back then: a prison of verbal and sometimes physical abuse. Was it any wonder he'd lived in the orchards, up at the big house, anywhere Abbey had been? He'd realized years ago that the Whittakers had kept his parents on long after they should have because of him. And they'd paid dearly for that kindness. He would never, ever stop trying to make up for it.

Arms slid around him from behind. He knew it was Abbey, even before she rested her cheek against his back. "Hey."

"Hey." He settled his arms over hers, feeling the warmth of her soak into him, and the knots inside him began to loosen.

"You okay?"

It was on the tip of his tongue to say yes. Because he'd grown accustomed to skating over the truth. But this was Abbey. "No. I just spoke to Davis."

He felt her stiffen. "Oh?"

"He claims he wasn't the leak."

"Do you believe him?"

Needing to see her for this, Kyle pivoted, pulling her close. "I think I actually do. Despite the lengths he's gone to over the years to protect his investment, violating an NDA to screw with me doesn't really make sense. He doesn't do things by halves. If he wanted to torpedo me, he'd have done a lot more than feed one tiny detail."

Her eyes searched his face. "So who?"

"Maybe no one. Not the way I was thinking. I've put so much effort into hiding my past, I guess I felt like it was a more deeply buried secret than it is. But anybody who connects me to this place—as they will through you—can find it."

When she started to pull away, he held on.

"No. Don't mistake me. I don't regret being here. I don't regret being with you. But I'd be lying if I didn't admit to being worried. What will my fans say when they find out that country music's Captain America is the son of a couple of felons? That everything I've done has been to outrun the stink of who I am?"

"That isn't who you are, Kyle."

His lips twisted in a bitter smile. "They don't know who I am. Not really. Image takes years to build and moments to destroy."

"Your fans—your true fans—are about your music. And it's not like huge numbers of people in this country don't have relatives involved with the justice system on some level or other. Everybody who commits a crime is related to somebody."

"It's not that. I don't actually think people will stop listening to my music because of where I came from. But you remember how bad it was here during and after the trial. People looking, whispering, making judgments about what I'd done, whether I was more involved. If everything comes out, it'll start all over again on a much bigger scale. And I don't know if I can deal with the shame of that."

As soon as the words were out of his mouth, he wished them unsaid. Verbalizing this fear felt like a self-fulfilling prophecy. But maybe it was too late to stop that.

Abbey's eyes were fierce as she reached up to frame his face. "I don't know how to get you to understand that shame only has power in the dark. If you bring it to light, it can't survive. You have *nothing* to be ashamed of. *Nothing.* You never did."

But being told—as he had been for years afterward—had never done anything to shake loose the shame that was so deeply embedded in his heart. It was why he hadn't ever tried to cross the line with Abbey in high school. Why he'd been driven to make something of himself. Why he'd simply accepted that she'd cut him off for years without a word. Because, deep down, he didn't feel worthy of her. He never had.

And there was a part of him that was waiting for her to figure that out for herself.

"Stop it." Her words were soft but full of heat. "Stop looking for the end of us when we're barely begun."

Kyle sucked in a breath. "Am I that transparent?"

"Did you forget that I know every shade of this face? Every look in your eyes? We may have missed a decade of experiences, but it doesn't change the fact that I *know* you. And I love you. I always have." She rose to her toes, brushing a quiet kiss over his lips. "Now be a good boy and let me."

Pulling her closer, he found her lips again. "As you wish."

ABBEY CRACKED open an eye and found daylight. That couldn't be right. Slapping her hand on the nightstand until she found her phone, she brought it close enough to read the time. After seven.

"Shit!"

Vaulting out of the bed she'd sadly had to herself, she moved from dresser to closet, grabbing up clean clothes and racing for the bathroom. She'd overslept and didn't even feel rested from it. That was, she supposed, what happened when you spent half the night awake, thinking about life-altering sex and wishing you could do it all over again.

Embracing the messy bun, she leapt into the shower, lathered up, rinsed off. Ten minutes after she'd rolled out of bed, she was dressed and as presentable as she was going to be for the day. Her clients hardly cared whether she had on full makeup or just mascara and blush. The scent of food and, more importantly, coffee drew her to the kitchen. As none of it smelled burned, she was banking on Kyle being the origin.

He stood barefoot at the stove, in jeans and

a soft, soft t-shirt that molded to his chest and shoulders in a way that had her mouth watering and her hands itching to trace them again. This whole picture could be a calendar. Sexy, thoughtful man makes breakfast. Affection, amusement, and attraction bumped together inside her like a trio of joyful, rough and tumble puppies. But the dark specter of regret sucked some of the life out of the scene. How many mornings like this could they have had if only they'd both fought harder?

He's here now. Don't spend this time thinking about what might have been.

Determined not to waste another moment, she crossed to him, laying one hand on his shoulder and stopping his automatic "Good morning" with a kiss. Soft, sweet. *I'm glad you're here. I'm glad you're mine.*

"Finally did something about that, huh? About damned time."

Abbey dropped back to her feet and pressed her lips together in mortification. She hadn't seen Granddaddy camped out at the kitchen table, which said a lot about her focus on Kyle. For his part, Kyle's blue eyes danced with laughter. The sight of it warmed her heart, made her feel like they shared a secret. They'd had so many growing up, and it was an intimacy she'd missed.

"Good morning, Granddaddy."

"Good for somebody anyway." He smirked over his coffee cup.

Oh my God. Was he implying... Nope. No way. Her brain was not going there. It violated the laws of her personal universe. She rejected this reality and substituted one of her own where her grandfather had not just casually remarked on her sex life. He wasn't supposed to know she *had* a sex life. Which... she hadn't since she moved home to Eden's Ridge.

"You want coffee?" Kyle asked.

More than my next breath. "I'll get some at the spa. We have an early meeting I forgot about, and I overslept."

"Take some breakfast, at least." Turning back to the stove, he quickly scooped some scrambled eggs onto a tortilla, added a couple strips of bacon and some cheese, and rolled it into a burrito. Wrapping the whole thing in a paper towel, he handed it over. "Portable."

"Well, aren't you handy?"

"Lots of experience eating on the go."

"Boy, don't you be giving away all my bacon."

Kyle pointed the spatula. "You want that bacon, you eat your fruit. That was the deal."

Granddaddy's chin jutted out in familiar defiance. Recognizing what was coming, Abbey opened her mouth to warn Kyle, but he just shooed her toward the door.

"I've got this."

"But—"

"You already said you're late. Get going."

Abbey hesitated. Kyle hadn't dealt with Granddaddy in one of his belligerent moods. And if he was starting out that way this early in the day, that didn't bode well. Maybe she should make some other arrangements.

"Abs, really. I've got this. If we need you, we'll let you know."

She had to trust somebody sometime. "I'll see you both later. Keep out of trouble!"

It felt weird to leave them there together and head off to work. Not that she hadn't been doing exactly that most of the past week, but today felt different. Because *they* were different. Now it wasn't a favor or some kind of exchange. Now it was... domestic. Family. They'd been a form of family for years, but this was something else. Something deeper. Richer.

Abbey was beyond grateful to have this opportunity with him, and she'd do anything she could to protect it. Which was why she was absolutely headed to work early to bust up in the middle of the weekly Reynolds family breakfast at The Misfit Inn, where all the sisters and an assortment of their respective spouses and children showed up to share a meal. Xander would probably be there. She needed to talk to him as Sheriff, and she preferred to do it in private rather than down at the station.

With the privilege of friendship, she let herself in through the front door of the inn and headed straight back to the kitchen. Whatever Athena was making smelled divine, as always. The din of voices grew louder as she stepped through the swinging door and into the familiar chaos. The benches around the massive farmhouse table were full, exactly as Kyle's foster mom, Joan, had liked it. If she'd lived, she'd have adored seeing Kennedy bouncing her chubby infant daughter Caroline, while a besotted Xander looked on. Pru's husband Flynn herded their toddler Bailey toward a highchair, while Pru herself had an intense discussion with Ari about... something or other. On the other side of the big island, Athena moved shoulder-to-shoulder with Dylan, the eldest of her two adopted boys, while the younger, Jesse, and her husband, Logan, carried platters to the table. The only no-shows for the morning appeared to be Maggie and Porter, with their infant daughter, Faith.

Perfectly at home, Abbey strode into the chaos and made a beeline for the coffeepot. She'd already grabbed a mug from the cabinet before anyone actually noticed her.

"Here to mooch?" Athena's tone lacked the bite it would've had before Logan. Love had mellowed her considerably.

Abbey slipped into the space that opened up between Ari and Pru and reached for one of the few big, fluffy biscuits remaining. "Partly. Is it so hard to believe I would like to enjoy y'all's delightful company?"

Athena, who'd seen her with Kyle when they'd picked up Granddaddy last night, just pursed her lips. Abbey wondered if she'd had their afternoon's activities tattooed all over her face.

Pru passed the butter. "Did you need a break from things with Kyle?"

"No." She'd come to talk to Xander. She considered waiting, trying to speak with him privately. But in the end, this would likely impact the entire family. They all needed to be aware of what could be coming. "Actually, I needed to ask our sheriff for a favor. In his professional capacity."

At the opposite end of the table, Xander sobered. "Are y'all having more trouble with the paparazzi?"

She shook her head. "No. I mean, not more than before. This is something else." For a moment, she hesitated. Kyle didn't want this information getting out. But this was his family, not the general public. *It's in the name of protecting him.*

"Kyle's mom is out of prison."

A burst of exclamations circled the table until she held up her hand for silence.

"I need you to find out whatever there is to find. When she got out. Where she's living. Presumably she's on parole. What are the terms of that?"

"You think she'll be out to cause trouble?"

"She showed up at his last concert. He

didn't speak to or acknowledge her, but she wants something. And I think after everything that happened, she'll absolutely feel like he owes her. I figure it's only a matter of time before she shows up here."

"You got it. I'll check on his dad, too."

"Thank you. It would help to have some idea what we're up against."

"We?" The surprise and skepticism in Kennedy's tone made her bristle.

"I'm not leaving him to face them alone." She'd been protecting him in big ways and small for most of their lives. No matter how long they'd been apart, that was still her natural inclination.

"So you're back to defending him?" Pru's tone was carefully neutral. Ever the peacemaker.

Well, she could hardly resent their incredulity when she'd bristled at the mere mention of Kyle's name for the past decade. Tearing off a piece of fluffy biscuit, she sucked in a bracing breath. "We finally talked and cleared the air about... before. It wasn't what I thought. It wasn't what either of us thought. Defending him is the least I can do for not giving him the chance to explain sooner."

The strain of denying her feelings was gone. Being able to release the burden of believing the worst of him was such an incredible relief. Deep down, a part of her had always known he wasn't that guy. The guilt over her own role in their time apart still weighed heavy, but she was more than willing to lay the blame where it truly belonged—on his snake-in-the-grass manager. They'd both been young and foolish, and he'd played them.

Joke's on you, Davis. We're together now, and I'm not letting him go again.

Athena tucked her tongue in cheek. "Judging by the look on the pair of you when you stopped by last night, clearing the air wasn't the only thing you did."

Abbey delivered a very polite, firm, "No comment," exactly as Deanna had trained her.

But her cheeks were on fire as she remembered their time in his loft.

Flynn shoved back from the table. "On that note, it's time to leave for school, *cailín beag*."

"But, Dad! We're just getting to the good part!" Ari protested.

"I'm sure someone will fill you in later. School. You too, boys. Grab your bookbags."

In the flurry of movement, Xander snagged the last biscuit. "I should get going, too. I want to check with the Tennessee Department of Corrections first thing."

"Thanks, Xander."

Logan made his excuses as well, and shortly, she was alone with her friends.

"Anybody notice how the boys always decamp when it's about time to do the dishes?" Pru observed.

"We'll get them back later," Kennedy assured her. "Let's not change the subject. Abbey's still in the hot seat here. What exactly does this mean for you and Kyle?"

Abbey instinctively ran her thumb over the

bottom of the engagement ring and considered. They hadn't discussed it in detail. Not yet. But she knew him. She understood him. There was only one path that made sense right now. "We're all in."

Pru folded her hands on the table. "Honey, are you sure? This is an awfully fast flip."

"It's really not. It's just… a very delayed inevitability. I agreed to this, knew I could sell it, because I'm not acting at all. Neither is he. If we were both less bullheaded, we'd have gotten here years ago."

"Where exactly *is* here?" Kennedy wanted to know. "Like… the fake engagement is a real one now?"

Abbey shrugged. "We haven't gotten that far yet. The whole point of that plan is kind of irrelevant now. It served its purpose—*his* purpose, anyway—and let him close enough to get me to listen. At the end of the day, we're together. Right now, that's good enough for me."

"Then I'd say it's good enough for the rest of us," Kennedy declared.

Pru lifted Bailey out of the highchair, accepting an enthusiastic toddler kiss. "I say it merits a family dinner. We need to bring Kyle back into the fold properly."

"Good food and razzing," Athena agreed. "It's a Reynolds family tradition."

CHAPTER 11

"Kyle, this is Rayna Dunham from Quicksilver Entertainment. The final numbers for the tour are in, and they are fantastic. We want to talk about contracts for your next albums. Between you and me, I think your next one will go platinum! Give me a call back and let us know when we can expect previews of what's coming next."

Kyle listened to the voicemail once more. He kept expecting to feel something at the knowledge that his label was so happy with

him. This was what he'd been working toward. The reason he'd endured six months on
the road with Mercy Lee and all her diva ten-
dencies. The motivation for every single time
he'd listened to Davis instead of his own gut
over the last ten years. Rayna had said albums,
plural. They didn't make those kinds of offers
to artists they didn't think could have major
star power. But all he felt was a vague anxiety
and a strong desire to hole up somewhere
without a way for them to contact him.

At least Davis wasn't around to make the
decision for him. Kyle knew he should probably do something about replacing his manager, but that could wait.

Abbey opened the passenger-side door and
hopped in. "I swear, those old men like to
gossip as much as teenage girls. Before I left,
Granddaddy was already asking Norm how
his campaign to talk Estelle Murchison into
marrying him was going."

Kyle slid the phone back into his pocket.
"You do realize the entire point of poker

games is for men to gossip over something that seems like a manly activity, right?"

"I'm getting that gist. Let's get on to the inn. I'm starving."

They made the short drive to the edge of town and down the winding, tree-lined drive that led to the three-story Victorian where Kyle had spent his teen years. Everything was different since Joan had died. Not that he'd been home for years before that. The girls had come back together, opened the inn, built the spa. They'd made a good place here, good lives. The house still held the comfort Joan had imbued it with, even if there was an extra layer of polish.

At the front door, Kyle hesitated. He no longer felt as if he had the right to just walk into this house where he used to live. These people had once been family. In Joan's world, they still were because chosen family stuck, and all those who'd gone through her home chose the family she'd offered. But he'd cut almost everybody off, aside from the handful of his other foster siblings who'd pursued life outside Eden's Ridge, and he hadn't come home, hadn't really responded to the overtures his sisters had made through the years. Abbey hadn't been the only one he'd hurt. He'd have to atone for that.

Abbey stroked a hand down his arm, lacing her fingers with his. "They won't bite."

"You sure?"

"Okay, much," she amended with a grin. She was the one who opened the door, dragging him inside and straight back toward the kitchen, where something smelled amazing.

Mealtimes here had always felt a little like a party. Joan had never been happier than when her long table was filled with her kids and their friends. Now those kids had kids of their own. Wasn't that a helluva thing? All his sisters and their spouses were present, wrangling their offspring. Griff was in one corner, chatting with Porter and Xander as they tossed two giggling babies from one person to the next. The din of conversation was ferocious and made him smile. At least until it died off at the sight of him.

Kyle braced himself. They'd been pissed at him for hurting Abbey, and definitely didn't approve of the fake engagement. How were they going to respond to the idea that he and Abbey were together for real? Would they even believe it?

Ari was the one who broke the silence with a fist pump. "I had less than a week in the pool."

Somebody groaned, "Dang it."

"The pool on what?" Kyle asked warily.

"On how long it would take a fake relationship to turn real." Her grin turned delighted. "Somebody else has my bathroom cleaning duty. Thanks for that."

Kyle had no idea what to say to that. "You're... welcome?"

Abbey laughed. "You'll get used to it. She opines about everybody's relationships."

"I'm usually right."

"Smug isn't a good look on you, sweetheart," Pru admonished.

"Oh, don't worry. We're *all* waiting for her to bring a guy home. She will absolutely reap what she's sown."

At Athena's promise, Ari's face went a little pale.

Kennedy smirked. "Two words: Cullen. Walker."

"Shut *up!*" Ari hissed.

"I'm just sayin'."

The two boys, who Kyle pegged as somewhere around ten and twelve, began to snicker.

"Dylan, Jesse, be careful who you tease. Retribution is a thing," Athena warned.

"Yes, Mom," they chorused.

He relaxed as the ribbing and razzing shifted into an old, familiar rhythm. This was home. It was welcome. One he wasn't sure he deserved but wouldn't take for granted.

Hands were washed. Wee ones were tucked into highchairs. Platters and bowls were carried to the table. Kyle found himself seated between Abbey and Dylan, Athena's eldest.

Once plates were filled, Kennedy raised a glass. "To Abbey and Kyle. Here's to clearing the air and bringing him back to the fold. Welcome home, brother."

A chorus of cheers circled the table. As they died down, Ari went chin in hands. "Well, I personally want to hear all about the tour. Was it fabulous? The lights? The crowds? Getting to see all those different places?"

"I hate to burst your bubble, kid, but touring is grueling. You're never in one place for more than a day or two, and never long enough to really take in the sights. It's this constant cycle of on the go. Don't get me wrong—the fans are great. Sharing my music is great. But the realities of touring are a very long way from fabulous."

"Understatement of the century," Griff muttered. "I thought the Marines could be a grind. I mean, not that it wasn't, but at least I got to drive cool vehicles and shoot big guns."

"You did, at least, have the benefit of *not* getting shot at on the road with me."

"Fair point," Griff conceded.

"I prefer my way," Flynn reflected. "I never had the fame, but I didn't want it. Not really."

Kyle's interest piqued as he studied Pru's husband. "You're a musician?"

"Oh, to be sure. Irish folk music mainly. I played my way through Ireland and across much of Europe, seeing a big chunk of the world on my own terms. It's part of how Kennedy and I met. I played a pub where she was tending bar. As she's a fine voice and a traveler's spirit, by week's end, she'd joined the band and gone with us as we made our way around Ireland."

"Ah, those were the days. And just think... if I hadn't done that, we never would've become friends, you wouldn't have come to visit me after I moved home, you wouldn't have met Pru, and we wouldn't have this little munchkin." Kennedy tweaked Bailey's button nose.

Bailey giggled.

"Do you miss it?"

"Oh, I keep my hand in. We host a weekly Jam Night here at the inn during the summers. And during cooler weather, we relocate to the Artisan's Guild."

"Jam Night?"

"It's exactly what it sounds like. Musicians from all over show up and just play and sing," Kennedy explained. "There have been some really interesting collaborations to come out of it. It's turned into a way bigger crowd than we'd initially anticipated, so there are folks who sell refreshments as fundraisers, but other than that it's all about the music for the joy of it."

Music simply for the joy of it? That sounded like heaven. "When's the next one?"

Maggie readjusted Faith in her baby sling. "Tomorrow, as it happens. Out at the Artisan Guild."

"Count me in. I love smaller venues." It would be nice to soak up some of the energy from musicians who just wanted to play.

Jesse eyed him dubiously. "Really? Aren't the big crowds and lights and stuff better?"

"I can and have done the big stadium shows. They're a rush for sure, and certainly there's more money there, which makes the label happy. But it also means that's all there is to my life. One of touring constantly, one show after another, until you get so mixed up, somebody has to write the name of the city on your hand, so you don't accidentally call out the wrong one at the start of the show. It's not conducive to creativity or creating *new* music."

Dylan narrowed his eyes, considering. "If you can't write new music, how do you get another album to tour for?"

"An excellent question. Some musicians don't write their own music. They perform songs other folks wrote. My last album had a few of those on it because I just... couldn't produce under those conditions. And I hated it. They were perfectly good songs, but they weren't *mine*. So I'm not doing that again. Which is why I'm dodging calls from my label. Partly, anyway."

"You wouldn't be the first of us to hide from a problem here." With a wry smile, Athena lifted her glass.

"Or find the answer," Maggie added. "What are you still committed to with your current label?"

"Nothing, actually. I haven't signed another contract with them yet, but after this last tour, they're talking a multi-album deal."

"Kyle, that's amazing," Pru exclaimed. "It's what you always wanted."

It had been. He'd left Eden's Ridge with an idea of not only making something of himself, but literally making himself over. Getting away from the bad parts of where he'd come from, who he'd believed he was. He'd done it with considerable success. But he'd also lost so much along the way. Family, friends, and the woman he loved.

Beside him, Abbey had gone still and stiff. And why shouldn't she? He'd just mentioned a multi-album deal. That meant more of those back-to-back tours that would take him away from her. He thought of what Davis had said. *Would all the sacrifices your career demanded have been too much?*

Kyle didn't want to think the man had been onto something. But he couldn't deny that nothing about the life he'd been living was conducive to a healthy relationship. It wasn't conducive to anything but a healthy bank account, and there was more to life than that.

"I don't know if I want it. Not at the terms I know they'll offer." There was something freeing about admitting it out loud, especially as he heard Abbey's slow, controlled exhale. They'd have things to discuss. But later, without the massive family audience.

Maggie's gaze turned speculative. "What kind of terms are you wanting?"

"More down time. The opportunity and space to create again. More stylistic freedom.

And the chance to actually *have* a family and personal life. A home. I've done the last decade without it, and I don't want to keep going down that road." He curled his fingers around Abbey's beneath the table, needing her to understand the truth of this.

"You don't think they'll go for that?" Kennedy asked.

"Well, I fired my manager, so I don't presently have anyone to negotiate for me."

"So get a new manager."

Ari's tone of duh had Kyle huffing a laugh. "It's not quite that simple. And either way, I've been tied up with things here."

Abbey spoke for the first time since the discussion began. "You're writing again since you came home."

Kyle met those big, dark eyes. "It seems I have a lot to say."

A smile fluttered at the corners of her mouth. "Then keep writing. Your music will give you more power at the negotiation table. If they want it, they'll wait. And if they don't, there will be others who do. You have the reputation to demand what you want now. So use it to build the life you want. Don't just accept the one someone else has forced on you."

After years of feeling like he had to bow to the whims of others, as he looked into Abbey's eyes, he finally felt like maybe she was right, and he could write his own future.

"Aren't you coming to bed, Ruthie?" Granddaddy had been cheerfully convinced Abbey was her grandmother since they'd picked him up from the poker game, probably because of all that talk of love and marriage and Norm's campaign to woo Estelle.

Heart squeezing, Abbey tucked him in, smoothing the covers over his frail body. "Not just yet. I want to do one of my puzzles first." She thanked God for her grandmother's life-long addiction to crossword puzzles before bed.

"Don't stay up too late."

"I won't." She bent and pressed a kiss to his brow, wanting to do what she could to soothe him and hoping he'd slide on in to sleep without remembering Grandma Ruth wasn't really here. "I love you, Roy."

"Love you, too, Ruthie girl."

Abbey switched off the lamp and quietly shut the door behind her.

Kyle was outside on the front porch, quietly picking out a melody on his guitar with the kind of stop-start rhythm that told her he was tinkering with a new song. His fingers didn't stop as she stepped out, and she found her head bobbing with the melody.

"He settle okay?"

"I think so. I'll check on him in a little while." Crossing to the railing, she leaned her shoulder against it and rubbed at the ache in her chest. "I think this is sometimes the hardest part of his condition, when he thinks I'm her and forgets she's been gone for eight years. He loved her so much, for so many years. And then his mind kicks back in, and he remembers… it's like watching him lose her all over again. I'm hoping he'll fall asleep before he hits that point tonight."

Kyle set his guitar aside. "Come here."

Needing the comfort, she slid into his lap, snuggling in. His arms came around her, and the ache relaxed a bit.

"Your grandparents were the greatest model for me for what I wanted in a relationship. Your parents, too. But what Granddaddy had with Grandma Ruth was just special."

"Yeah." Growing up around them, it had been hard not to use that relationship as the yardstick for everything. Was it any wonder the few others she'd tried had been lacking?

"I always thought we were like them," he admitted. "God knew, I wanted to be."

"So did I." Abbey pressed her cheek to the scruff of his. "You never thought you deserved me."

"I got told that often enough by my parents."

Abbey growled. "I hate your parents. For so very many reasons."

"Me, too."

Remembering the news Xander had passed on before she left the inn, she bit her lip. "I did a thing. You might be pissed about it."

"What did you do?" His tone indicated he wasn't worried about whatever it was.

"I had Xander check on your parents."

He stiffened for a moment, then let out a slow breath. "I probably should have asked myself."

Straightening, she curved a hand around his nape, as if that would somehow make the conversation easier. "I know you don't want to think about it, but forewarned is forearmed."

"True enough. What did he find out?"

"Your dad isn't getting out any time soon. He's had some behavioral issues inside that added time to his sentence. Your mom was released three weeks ago and is currently living in a halfway house in Nashville. He's keeping in touch with her parole officer."

He nodded and blew out another breath. "Okay. Thanks for finding out. At least it's just her I have to worry about."

"We. You're not in this alone." She'd keep reminding him until he believed it.

Eyes searching her face, he leaned forward to kiss her temple. "I love you, Abbey."

Her heart swelled. They'd always been affectionate, always said I love you. It had been important to her and her family that he knew it growing up because he sure as hell wasn't getting it at home. But it was different, knowing this wasn't simply friendship. This was what she used to call the big L kind of love. Different and terrifying.

"Did you mean what you said? About not wanting the big contracts?" She hadn't meant to say it. But it had been on her mind since dinner. They'd only just found their way back to each other, and this was the thing that could rip him away from her again.

If he was perturbed by the question, he didn't show it. "I'd love the distribution and support. But, if I agree to a multi-album deal, they own me until I deliver on all of them. The cage will be more gilded, but it's still a cage. I don't want that. More, I don't want you to have to deal with that. Nothing about that life would be fair to you."

Abbey didn't disagree. And yet… "I don't want you giving up your dreams for me." She hesitated before voicing the truth that had been kicking around her brain. "I think maybe you would have if we'd gotten married back when." Because she wouldn't have been able to stand it, him being gone all the time. And life on the road simply wouldn't have been an option for her.

Kyle traced a finger along her brow, down her cheek. "Dreams change. When I was here as a kid, all I wanted was to go. When I left, all I could dream about was you. This chance with you *is* my dream, and I'm not willing to give it up for anything."

Her heart rolled over in her chest. "Kyle."

So long ago, she'd locked away her dreams

of a life with him. As she pressed her lips to his, the lid cracked open and those hopes and fantasies crept out, reaching for him. A part of her wanted to pull them back, tuck them away again where they'd be safe. But where had that gotten her? Cut off from her best friend and the love of her life for a decade? Wasn't it better to be brave and reach for what she'd always wanted? He was worth the risk. And she owed it to both of them to believe in him and them.

Easing back, she pressed her brow to his. "How are we going to make this work?"

"I don't know. But a wise woman told me the power is in my hands. I just have to use it." He kneaded her nape with strong fingers. "No one ever believed in me like you do."

If she'd so fully believed in him, would they have spent the past ten years not talking? Shoving away the guilt, she kept her tone light. "Just calling it like I see it."

"I like how you see it."

Relaxing into him again, she tipped her

head to his shoulder. "If you could build exactly the career you wanted, what would it look like?"

"More small venues. Intimate shows, without all the glitz and glam, where the focus is on the music, not the production value. Nothing but my own music. Time and space to write it. And I'd like to have time to give back to at-risk kids. I would have turned out a lot different without your family. Without Joan. I want to be able to do that without my label wanting to make it a publicity stunt."

"None of that seems like too big an ask." It wasn't about more money or more fame. That had never been what drove him.

"We'll see, I guess." He shifted his fingers from her nape to her shoulder, kneading the knots that seemed like permanent residents there. "What about you? What do you want?"

What *did* she want? When was the last time anyone had asked her that?

"I don't know. Moving back home was never the plan. But my parents needed help, and I certainly don't begrudge them that. I'm grateful to get this extra time with Grand-daddy. Plus, coming back to the Ridge and opening the spa has been great. I love what we've built there, and I get to work with my best friends every day. I'm happy here in a way I didn't think I'd be. But I guess I want the chance for more room for me. I'm not used to thinking about that anymore."

"You never were. You always put others first. I can't remember a single time you were selfish that didn't involve eating all the straw-berry Sour Patch Kids."

She laughed and trailed her fingers down his chest, enjoying his shiver at her touch. "I'm feeling selfish with you. I don't want to share you. And I'm sorry we've had all these other responsibilities and the lack of privacy."

"I like being able to help. Though I'd be lying if I didn't admit I've been thinking about getting you naked again."

At his words, her thighs went loose, and

heat pooled low in her belly. "I want you in my bed."

His eyes lit with mischief and an erotic intent. "Can you be quiet?"

"Once Granddaddy takes his hearing aids out, he wouldn't hear a nuclear bomb."

"Do we know he's asleep?"

"One way to find out."

Abbey slid off his lap, taking his hand and leading him inside. They heard the snoring from Granddaddy's room before they'd made it two steps into the house. Even so, they crept upstairs. There was something deliciously forbidden about dragging him up to her childhood bedroom. She instinctively avoided the squeaky steps and floorboards on the way. Not that she'd have been able to hear them over the thrumming of her own heartbeat.

Kyle was the one who shut and locked the door behind them. "Gotta admit, it's a little weird, the idea of being with you here."

Understanding, she linked her arms around his neck. "At least I don't still have my poster of Aragorn smoldering at us from the ceiling." She hadn't made that many more adjustments to the space since moving home. New bedding, an extra bookcase. But her trim little laptop sat on the same desk where she'd done homework for school, and the window seat where she and Kyle had wedged themselves in to talk of anything and everything still had the same plaid cushion.

He stroked his hands down her torso. "I know they're on a cruise, but there's a part of me that's still paranoid your dad will come barging in with a shotgun."

Abbey laughed. "There shall be no parental interruptus, and that's not Dad's style, anyway."

Kyle grimaced. "Maybe let's stop talking about your parents."

"Maybe let's stop talking at all." She tipped her face up to his and proved she could stay quiet after all.

CHAPTER 12

Strategically placed spotlights illuminated the stone walls and beams of the old mill that now housed the Artisan Guild. Though "old" no longer seemed to apply as a descriptor. The last time Kyle had been out here had been on a hike when they were in high school. There'd been vines and overgrowth and an ineffable abandoned air that had given rise to ghost stories to explain why the place had been abandoned nearly a century before. That had certainly been cooler than the truth—that the rerouting of the river that powered the mill had put it out of business, toppling the empire of Joan's lumber baron ancestor.

The place certainly wasn't abandoned now. Dozens of cars filled the parking lot, and people streamed toward the front doors, many with assorted instruments in hand.

Kyle gawked for a moment until a car behind him gave a little honk to get moving again.

"Wow. I don't know what I expected, but this wasn't it."

Abbey grinned. "Impressive, isn't it? Maggie and Porter do good work. She had the idea to turn the property into the Artisan Guild headquarters. Porter made it a reality."

The complex was huge, with an addition jutting off to one side that looked every bit a part of the original nineteenth-century structure.

"What do they even do out here, other than Jam Night?"

"There's a maker's space, with shared tools

and equipment, so different kinds of artisans can ply their crafts, and also plenty of classrooms so they can teach. Maggie wanted to create something that would keep those skills from dying out and be a draw for tourism to the area. Which it has been. And, of course, there's retail space so those same artisans can sell their wares."

"That Maggie Reynolds was always a smart cookie," Granddaddy declared.

"Yes, she is." Kyle pulled up to the wide double doors and threw the Land Cruiser into park.

Before he could do more than tug open the rear passenger door, Granddaddy was sliding out, eager to get inside. Thank God he was down to a single crutch.

Abbey hurried around, sliding an arm coquettishly through his in a gesture as much of affection as stability. "Hold up, now. You're not gonna go running in there without your date, are you?"

Granddaddy beamed. "Prettiest girl at the party."

Taking in her fall of straight blonde hair and the flush of pleasure in her cheeks, Kyle had to agree. "I'll go park and come find you."

"Look for your sisters. They'll have camped out near the action."

As Kyle drove on down the hill, searching for a space in the wider lot below, his phone began to ring. One glance at the readout on his dashboard had him grimacing and ignoring the call. He wasn't talking to anybody from the label tonight. But he did check the voicemail as he strode back toward the entrance to the mill.

"Kyle, this is Rayna Dunham again. I know you're enjoying some well-earned downtime, but we really want to get you to the negotiating table. We heard about your split with Davis. Don't let that deter you. We still absolutely want to talk. We also wanted to let you know that there's an opportunity for you to sing at the Ryman in two weeks. Thomas

Rhett had to cancel, and they want *you*. I know I don't have to tell you what a big feather that would be in your cap. Call me back!"

The Ryman Auditorium. The Mother Church of Country Music. Original home of the Grand Old Opry. The stage where country greats from Johnny Cash to Patsy Cline had sung. It *was* a hell of an opportunity.

But he didn't call back. That was the cheese they'd use to lure him in before springing the trap. He wasn't ready for that conversation. Tonight was for music and friends and family. He wanted to be present in more than just body, not with his head all tied up, worrying about the future.

Joining the throngs, he filed inside. Just beyond a vestibule lined with black and white photos of the original mill, the space opened into a massive, high-ceilinged room. The perimeter was lined with what looked like workstations, housing all manner of tools and equipment. The maker's space that Abbey had mentioned. At the far end, chairs were clustered in a horseshoe, with musicians settling in, unpacking their instruments. The audience was a seething, cheerful mass of lawn chairs, blankets, and coolers, broken up here and there by the lines of people snaking out from the food and beverage vendors set up along one wall. He spotted signs for high school clubs and church groups raising money for one cause or another, selling popcorn or hotdogs or whatever could be brought in and easily kept warm or cold for the masses. It was a helluva setup.

His family had carved out a big section right up by the musicians. Granddaddy had a chair already and was bouncing Kennedy and Xander's daughter, Caroline, on his good knee, looking happy as a clam. The sight gave Kyle pause. Did Granddaddy want great-grandchildren? He'd been smitten with Abbey basically always, so it stood to reason he'd be delighted if she had children. Did *she* want kids? He didn't know. She'd always said she did when they were younger, but he knew plenty of folks who'd changed their minds as adults. It was another of those million and one details they hadn't yet had time to discuss about the future they were still finding the shape of. As she ran a gentle finger over the white-blonde down on Faith's head where it peeked out of the baby sling Maggie wore, Kyle found himself hoping she hadn't changed her mind.

"—got a call from Wyatt Sullivan the other day," Athena said. "You remember him from the reunion last fall? He got adopted when he was twelve."

Maggie patted a soft hand against Faith's back. "Sure. He mostly crossed over with me and Pru. That was before you came to us."

"I thought it was something like that. Anyway, he was asking for suggestions on his YouTube channel. Apparently he's got an eye to pitch for an actual show."

Kennedy perked with interest. "Yeah? What kind of concept?"

"Home improvement. Flips and stuff. His channel's called *DIWyatt*."

"Clever," Abbey murmured. "Is he any good?"

"As a contractor, definitely. I didn't have time to watch much, but it looks like he does really good work. And he's definitely got the looks for a TV home improvement guy."

Kyle joined them, sliding an arm around Abbey's waist and loving that she leaned into him. "And exactly what does a TV home improvement guy look like?"

Abbey's lips quirked in amusement. "She means he's hot. Which, yeah. He is. I met him at the reunion."

"Uh huh. Shall we go get everybody drinks?"

She laughed and patted his chest. "Smooth. But sure. What's everybody want?"

With multiple orders for cider, he and Abbey got in line for the booth from Forbidden Fruit Cidery. Kyle wondered if the owners would be manning it. He hoped they'd keep their mouths shut if they were. Ryder and his husband Lewis both brightened at the sight of him, circling around their little table to pull him into a back-slapping hug.

"Damn, it's good to see you home," Ryder declared.

"It's good to be home." Kyle was surprised to realize he meant it beyond the joy of being with Abbey. He'd enjoyed being back in Eden's Ridge. "And it's great to see you two looking so happy."

Lewis grinned. "If you love your work, you'll never work a day in your life. Am I right?" He clearly expected Kyle's agreement.

"So they say."

Ryder swung an arm around Lewis's shoulders. "Bonus points if you get to do that work with the love of your life."

Abbey gave a dreamy sigh. "You two are freaking adorable."

The two men were great together, and Kyle was delighted they'd managed to bring their dream of opening a cidery to full fruition, as it were.

"Talk about adorable. What about the two of *you*, Miss I-Kept-The-Biggest-Secret-The-Ridge-Has-Seen-Since-Us? Let's see the ring," Lewis demanded.

Abbey dutifully held out her hand. For a moment, Kyle wondered whether he should buy another. One more befitting what he could afford with his current success. But Lewis just pressed a hand to his heart. "It's so perfectly you."

She cut a glance in Kyle's direction, her lips curving into a warm smile. "Yes, it is. He did good."

"He's a good one," Ryder agreed.

Uncomfortable with the praise, Kyle decided they needed to get a move on. "Can we get a round of ciders for the group?"

"Sure thing. How many?"

He gave the order, and Ryder began to put them into a box to carry. Kyle pulled out his wallet to pay.

"Oh, hell no. Your money is no good here. By rights, these are part yours," Lewis insisted.

Kyle began making a slashing motion across his throat, but neither of them seemed to see.

"Why's that?" Abbey asked.

"Because he's our partner in the cidery," Ryder explained. "His investment is how we were able to buy the stake in the orchard to get started."

Her mouth dropped open, and she turned to stare at him.

The guys seemed to clue in that this was news to her.

"Um… was that still a secret?" Lewis asked.

Kyle forced a smile. "It's fine. But we'll take those ciders now. Got thirsty family." He hefted the box and turned without looking at Abbey.

She caught up to him in three strides. "You helped them buy part of the orchard so they could start Forbidden Fruit?"

"It was an investment opportunity."

Her hand on his arm finally made him stop. "Kyle. Look at me."

Bracing himself, he turned to meet her gaze. He didn't know what he wanted to see. Not the gratitude making those big doe eyes glimmer.

"That deal saved my family's business."

He jerked a shoulder. "It was a good investment all around."

"Don't downplay this. You saved our business. Our home. And I wasn't even speaking to you at the time. I don't even know how..." She swallowed. "And you kept it quiet all this time?"

He wished it were still a secret. But it wasn't, and he had to deal with that. "I know you and your family never blamed me for my parents' actions and that you don't think it's my job to make up for it, but I needed to do something to help, to pay restitution. Because they never will." So, he'd sunk almost all his profits from that first album that went gold into helping Ryder and Lewis start Forbidden

Fruit and keeping the orchard afloat the only way he knew how.

Her throat worked, and she looked perilously close to tears. "Thank you."

That tremulous tone made him itch to run. He didn't deserve thanks for this. It was the bare minimum of what her family deserved. There shouldn't be prizes for that.

Needing some space from her gratitude, he hurried back to his family, dropping off the drinks and grabbing his guitar to go join the other musicians.

He'd lose himself in the music until he felt in control again. Until he felt worthy again.

ABBEY WATCHED Kyle carry his guitar over to the cluster of musicians. He'd come here to play tonight, but she knew, in this moment, he was running away from her. From her gratitude.

Her own head was reeling. If not for his

investment in the cidery, they'd likely have lost their orchards entirely, and maybe the house as well. Her parents had never told her the bald numbers, but they'd been struggling for years because of what Kyle's parents had done, everything they'd taken. It would have happened sooner, probably, if Kyle himself hadn't found out and blown the whistle on the embezzlement. At thirteen, he'd chosen her family over his own, and his testimony had been the lynchpin in the case that sent his parents to prison. Despite that, he'd always had the notion that he was responsible for paying for their mistakes.

It seemed he'd finally found a way to do it, and Abbey didn't know what to do with that information. Would it be enough to make him feel worthy? To absolve him of the guilt he'd carried for so long?

"Sit right here with me, Butter Bean."

Grateful for the distraction, Abbey took the chair beside Granddaddy, sliding her arm through his and tipping her head to his shoulder as the assembled musicians launched into a rendition of "Tennessee Whiskey".

He laid his free hand over hers. "So is it real now?"

"Is what real?"

One gnarled finger traced over her ring. "The engagement."

Startled, she straightened to stare at her grandfather. They hadn't told him about it at all. He'd been deliberately excluded from the family meeting for fear he wouldn't be able to keep the secret. "How did you know... about any of it?"

"Psh. It was my idea. You didn't really think he came up with that on his own, did you? He'd never have taken that leap without being pushed."

Abbey stared at her grandfather. "You convinced him to convince me that a fake engagement was the only way to deal with the press?"

"Desperate times called for desperate measures." Granddaddy squeezed her hand. "I want you to have the kind of happy I was with my Ruthie. I saw the seeds of that with you and Kyle when you were children, but then everything got messed up. If somebody didn't intervene, you two were going to blow it."

Moved and more than a little flummoxed, Abbey leaned in to press a kiss to his wrinkled cheek. "Thank you for being a sneaky, sneaky man."

Granddaddy rumbled a laugh, and they settled in to enjoy the music. It was a round-robin style performance, with musicians hopping in and out, depending on whether they knew the song or not. They trotted out old standards like "Rocky Top", "Ring of Fire", and Diamond Rio's "Meet in The Middle". By the time Flynn coaxed out the opening notes to "The Devil Went Down to Georgia," Abbey could see Kyle unwinding enough to really sink into the performance and enjoy himself.

He didn't automatically hog the spotlight, instead gravitating to harmonies and supporting rhythms that showed off the skill of the other musicians present. But as he jammed with Flynn, sang with Kennedy, and hammed it up with Ari, Abbey saw the joy shining in his face. From what he'd told her, he hadn't had a great deal of that since he started pursuing professional music. She wanted him to get out of his career what Lewis and Ryder had managed with Forbidden Fruit. She wanted him to really, truly love what he did and recognize that he had value beyond the money he made, beyond whatever restitution he felt like he still needed to pay.

"Is that Kyle Keenan?"

Abbey looked over at the man who'd taken the next seat, a plate of empanadas in his lap. Dimly, she recognized him as one of the guests who'd recently arrived at the inn. "Yes, it is."

"This isn't what I expected of him. He's got a lot more versatility beyond what he's been allowed to do in Nashville."

"He's always been an extremely talented musician."

"Known him a long time?"

"All my life."

The guy turned to look at her. "You're the fiancée. Abbey, right? I'm Harry Cafferty."

She tensed, hesitating.

Harry lifted his hand and made a little X over his heart. "Not a reporter. Promise."

"That's what a lot of the reporters have said."

"Fair point. I'm just here to listen to the music."

Abbey hoped that was true.

They both joined in the applause as the latest song ended.

Kyle met her gaze across the room, grinning as he began to pick out the opening bars to one of the duets they used to sing together. He lifted his brows in invitation. Abbey frowned, pointing to herself. Kyle nodded. He wanted her to come sing with him? Was he out of his mind? The idea of it had her heart pounding like a timpani drum. He knew she couldn't sing in front of people. She'd never *really* sung in front of anyone but him.

She shook her head, mouthing an emphatic, "No."

Blowing her a kiss, he let it go. As someone else joined in, Abbey felt a little twinge, wishing she were brave enough to put herself out there. But she wasn't a performer. Never had been. Singing with Kyle had always been a private, intimate thing. She couldn't bring herself to overcome the paralyzing stage fright.

Before someone else could start the next song, Kyle spoke up. "I've been working on some new material lately. Would y'all be willing to indulge me and let me try it out?"

The audience whooped and hollered in approval.

"This is 'Bubble Gum Ring.'"

He began to strum a more complex version of one of the melodies she'd heard him fiddling with over the past week. It was a different sound than the music he'd recorded, and as he fixed his gaze on hers and began to sing, his rich baritone filling the space, gooseflesh broke out along Abbey's arms.

It was them. Their story. All the good parts. The childhood marriage pact with a bubble gum ring. The teenagers too afraid to act on their feelings. The adults who got a second chance. Each refrain came back to that plastic ring that had meant so much to them both.

"This is good," Harry muttered. "Very, very good."

But Abbey barely heard him. She couldn't focus on anything but Kyle and this very public gift he was giving her. It was a claiming, an acknowledgment, that had nothing to do with maintaining a fiction and everything to do with celebrating what had brought them together in the first place.

When he'd finished, the room erupted in applause. She felt the thunder of it as she rose from her chair and crossed to him. A part of her was aware that multiple people were recording from their phones. The performance and what came after would undoubtedly end up on YouTube and social media before the end of the night. But she didn't care. She really had to kiss him right now.

He was grinning as she captured his mouth to hoots and cheers. The growl in the back of his throat was a heady drug that made her wish for a helluva lot more privacy. But she'd settle for this public claiming of her own.

Kyle snagged her wrist as she pulled back. "Don't you run away after a kiss like that."

"Wouldn't dream of it." She couldn't even mind that she was breathless. He was worth it.

"You about made me drop my guitar."

Abbey grinned. "Now that would be a real shame. You play it so pretty."

"Always for you." He brought her hand to his lips and lavished a kiss on her knuckles.

Laughing, blushing, she broke eye contact, sweeping her gaze around the room to remind herself of their audience. All eyes were on them, which just made her blush harder. But the weight of one particular woman felt heavier. Drawn by the sensation, she glanced over in time to see her turning away. Abbey didn't recognize her, yet something in the way she moved was familiar. Maybe a guest or someone else's client at the spa?

Before she could pursue the thought, Ari was interrupting, linking her arm through Abbey's. "Excuse me, but if you two are finished making googly eyes at each other, some of us are here to play."

Abbey looked askance in her direction. "You live for the googly eyes."

"I'm thinking she's trying to distract us from the ones she's making at the dude manning one of the fundraiser tables," Kyle murmured.

Following his line of sight, Abbey saw the infamous Cullen Walker. "Ah ha."

"Psh. Whatever." Ari punctuated the statement with a dramatic teenage eye roll, but she couldn't stop the blush from staining her cheeks.

Willing to rescue the girl, Abbey patted her

arm and held out a hand for Kyle. "How about you take a break and come get some food? I'd like to spend some actual time with my date."

"Your wish is my command."

With a simpering smile, she winked. "I'll try not to let that go to my head."

CHAPTER 13

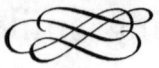

"Over two hundred thousand views since *last night!* And that's just this video. There are a bunch of others."

From his seat in one of the chairs on the front porch, Kyle grinned at Granddaddy's enthusiasm. Abbey had taught him how to look stuff up on YouTube on his phone at breakfast, and he'd promptly found the many videos of last night's unofficial debut of "Bubble Gum Ring" at Jam Night.

"Well, my publicist will sure be happy." He should probably call Deanna and give her a heads up. Then again, she kept her finger on social media and probably already had alerts set up.

"More to the point, *you* look happy."

"I reckon that's because I am. I've got a second chance with the best girl in the world. Everything else is just details." Details he knew he needed to sort out. But the music was flowing, and he didn't want to do anything to scare it off.

"I told you the plan would work."

Kyle chuckled. "So you did." He'd had his doubts, but it was hard to argue with the end result. He felt fantastic about where he and Abbey were.

"Speaking of details, when are you gonna make it official for real and ask that girl to marry you?"

The guitar made a discordant squawk as his fingers missed their position on the fret-board. "It's too soon for that. Way too fast. We *just* got together."

Granddaddy slapped the arm of his chair.

"Boy, you've wasted enough time. It's not an issue of fast when it's right. Now's when you make up for lost time. I'm not getting any younger, and I wanna see my girl go down the aisle."

Kyle wanted to tease and say he'd live till he was a hundred, but with his condition, that was unlikely to be the case. So instead, he considered what Granddaddy was saying. "It happens, I've had a few thoughts on the matter of how I'd propose." Hell, he'd more or less laid it out in that last interview. Would it mean more to her if he went that route, or should he try to come up with something new?

Before Granddaddy could offer any suggestions on the matter, the sound of a car coming up the drive drew their attention.

Kyle set his guitar aside. "It's too early for Abbey to be getting home from work. She's got clients until noon."

He rose from his seat, trotting on down the steps. It was probably somebody looking for the cidery who'd taken the wrong turn. He'd just give the driver directions.

But his step hitched as he caught sight of the woman behind the wheel.

No.

A mix of panic and fury swirled in his gut, driving him the rest of the way across the yard to where the little tin can of a car had rolled to a stop. She was already opening the door before he could slap a hand against it to keep her inside.

She unfolded from the seat, a bird-thin woman who looked decades older than she had when she'd gone into prison. Her hair was more gray than sandy now, thin and stringy. She was more than a head shorter than him, but that didn't make her presence any less of a threat.

She couldn't be here. She'd already done enough damage to this place, these people, and Kyle didn't want her anywhere near Grandaddy.

Because his hands shook, he curled them

into fists. "You get back in that car and get the hell off this property."

"Is that any way to greet your mother?"

"You're nothing to me." She'd been no kind of mother, and thanks to Faye Whittaker and Joan Reynolds, he had occasion to know the difference.

"I gave you life, and you'll show me the respect I'm owed," she snapped.

"Respect has to be earned, and you sure as hell never did anything to deserve it."

"Fed and clothed you, didn't I? Put a roof over your head."

"The Whittakers were more responsible for that than you ever were."

Twyla sneered. "Oh, the high and mighty Whittakers. You always did think you were one of them. Hanging out with that girl always gave you airs. As if you were ever good enough for the likes of them. You're no better than your daddy and me."

"I'm nothing like either of you." He'd spent

a lifetime eradicating any traces of his true origins.

"Blood will tell. Blood always tells. You can change your name and how you dress and talk, but that's all an act. You can't change what's down deep inside."

"You aren't welcome here. Get in your car and go."

"I got every right to come back. To see my son. You never even visited me in prison."

"Why would I? So you could berate me from behind bars? Belittle me from the other side of the plexiglass? You never wanted me. Don't pretend otherwise."

"Always so eager to get rid of us." A cold fury flashed across her face. "Always choosing them over your own kin. You owe us for that."

Kyle didn't like the calculating gleam in her eyes. "I don't owe you a damned thing."

"You've made good for yourself. A good son would share the rewards of his success. Especially after what you did to us."

"Keep dreaming."

"You've gone to all this trouble to keep everything quiet. What would all those fans of yours say if they knew what you really came from?"

His stomach lurched at the implied threat. She could ruin everything. It was what she did. And he'd built his entire career, his life, knowing it was a house of cards. But he'd thought he would have more time. And maybe the years had made him feel as if he had more control than he really did. But when had he ever actually had control over this woman?

As panic tried to claw up his throat, he remembered what Abbey had said and relaxed a fraction. He had more control than he thought. "My fans aren't a concern. They're in it for the music and you can't touch that. You won't get a penny out of me."

Dropping any prevarication, Twyla firmed her jaw. "You'll pay, or I'll go to the press. Tell them everything."

The idea of it terrified him. But Kyle understood that if he gave in to her demands and paid her once, it would establish a pattern that would never end so long as both his parents were living. They'd always think he owed them something, and he wasn't locking himself into that kind of devil's bargain. Besides, she couldn't be ready to act. She'd leave here, lick her wounds, maybe consult with his father. Then she'd be back with some other offer. It wasn't her pattern to choose the nuclear option first. His daddy had always been the decisive one.

"You'll get nothing from me but a boot up the ass."

"Get off my property." Granddaddy's voice shook with rage.

Kyle swung around to find him standing just a few feet away, arm draped over one crutch. His face was an alarming shade of red.

"Hello, Roy."

"Don't you hello me, you harpy. You get the hell away from here. You got no business coming back here." He hobbled forward, and

264 | KAIT NOLAN

Kyle leapt close to keep him from toppling on shaky legs.

"I've got this, Granddaddy."

But Granddaddy ignored him. All his focus was on Twyla. "You were terrible employees. Terrible parents. You never treated Kyle right. Never loved him the way you should."

"How we raised our boy was no business of yours."

Granddaddy raised his crutch, as if about to strike out with it. Kyle snagged it before he could swing. That was the last thing they needed. His mother would absolutely press assault charges.

Before anybody could say another word, another car came up the drive. Kyle recognized the sound of Abbey's Honda before it came over the hill and into view.

Twyla apparently decided adding someone else to the mix was too much because she edged back toward her own car. "Think about it. I'll be in touch."

Abbey skidded to a halt in the middle of

the driveway and leapt out, racing toward them. But Twyla was already in the driver's seat and backing up.

Granddaddy waved his crutch, shouting incoherent threats after her as she drove away.

"What the actual hell is she doing here?"

"Not now, Abs." Kyle had his hand on Granddaddy, doing his best to keep him stable. He didn't like the older man's pallor. "We need to get him inside and calmed down."

Evidently realizing there was nothing more to be done about Twyla, Abbey turned her attention to her grandfather. Together they got him back inside and into the recliner. As soon as he was settled, Kyle paced away, desperate to find some distance and control.

ABBEY QUIETLY SHUT the door to Granddaddy's room. The entire encounter had left him drained, and she hoped he'd nap for a while. If they were lucky, he'd have forgotten Kyle's mother by the time he surfaced. If they weren't... well, they'd deal with it. For now, she needed to do damage control with Kyle himself.

But she took a moment in the hall to slow her breathing and find some calm. She was more than a little rattled herself to have Twyla back in their lives. This woman was one of the two people who'd all but ruined her family. There was little Twyla could do directly to them now, but she could still attack Kyle. The woman knew exactly how to stomp all over his insecurities. She'd created them, after all. Abbey knew that, in whatever time she was here, Twyla probably slid right back into those toxic patterns, attacking his worth, stoking his shame. She just had to hope that her own hold over him was stronger.

Kyle stood in the living room, knocking back a glass of some kind of alcohol. It was barely past one in the afternoon. He glanced at her as she came into the room. "I'm sorry."

Her gut clenched as she wondered exactly

what he was apologizing for. The resolute lines of his face said he'd made some kind of decision. She was terrified it would be about them. But she kept her tone quiet and neutral. "For?"

"This is all my fault. She would never have come here if not for me. Granddaddy didn't need that. He could've been hurt—or worse— trying to protect the child I used to be."

Relaxing a bit, she crossed over and took the glass from his hand, sipping at the amber liquid herself. The bitter smoke of whiskey hit her tongue, and she grimaced. "This wasn't all about your mother. We've been really fortunate since you've been here that he's had mostly good days. This is one of the bad. They happen sometimes. You've just never seen it before. That doesn't mean it was your fault."

"He was fine before she got here. I should have been able to keep her away, but I just never thought she'd dare show her face here again. My mistake."

Abbey set the glass on the coffee table as

she thought of the woman she'd seen in the crowd last night. "I think she was at Jam Night."

His eyes widened. "What?"

"I didn't realize it was her. But I don't know what I could have done if I had. There's no law against attending a public event, and neither of us would have wanted a scene there." But at least they might have been fore-warned that Twyla was in the area. Too late now.

Kyle's shoulders were rigid, and a muscle ticked in his jaw. His blue eyes were arctic, and Abbey felt like he was oceans away in-stead of a hand span.

"What did she want?"

"Money. And maybe to see how much she could rattle me. Or us."

Mission accomplished on that front. "You can't pay her."

"I know. I told her as much. She threatened to go to the press and tell everything."

Which was exactly what he was afraid of.

Abbey had done her best to mitigate that fear. But she didn't know what was he willing to do in order to protect his reputation. "What did you say?"

"I called her bluff. Told her she wouldn't get a dime."

"Do you think she'll really do it?"

"Not immediately. She'll come back with another offer. More threats. Even if she went to the press, nobody's going to run the story without confirming that she's actually my mother." He turned away, pacing to the window to look out, but Abbey didn't think he actually saw the orchards beyond. "I should have enough time to craft something myself. I'll need to talk to Deanna. Figure out the best way to handle it."

"You're going to beat her to the punch?" She hadn't imagined he'd take that risk.

"I don't see any other alternative. The public will remember what they hear first, not what's necessarily true. That's why scandal endures so fucking long."

Old, familiar shame swirled around him, bowing those broad shoulders, dragging him away from her.

Screw that. She'd promised to call him out on bullshit, and this certainly qualified.

Abbey crossed over, sliding in front of him so he had to look down at her. "Look, this sucks. Nobody's saying it doesn't. But you're not alone in this."

"I don't want this blowing back on you or your family."

"If it does, it does. The law is on our side. The evidence is damning to both of them. It's why they were put away so long. There's no version of this story where you didn't do the right thing."

"It's not like I think I should have done anything different. I just... What do I have to do to be free of her? Of both of them?"

"I don't know. But no matter what, you have to remember I love you." She slid her arms around him. "We're in this together."

He finally, *finally* focused back in on her,

drawing her close and pressing his brow to hers. "I love you, Abbey."

"We're going to get through this, okay?"

"Okay." Sliding a hand into her hair, he brushed his lips over hers.

Abbey rose to him, wanting him to feel how much he meant to her. She wasn't letting him go again. Wouldn't let his parents or anything else come between them.

"Oh, my."

Startled, Abbey broke the kiss, turning her head toward the voice. "Mom? Dad?"

Her parents stood in the doorway to the kitchen, mouths agape. Faye had one hand pressed to her throat, and Mark's eyebrows were near his hairline. And why shouldn't they be shocked? When they'd left for their cruise, she'd been here on her own. She'd been angry with Kyle for years, for reasons they knew nothing about. And now they were home, and Kyle was here, and they were so clearly involved.

"You're home!" God, how could she have

forgotten they were due back in port today? Heat suffusing her cheeks, Abbey eased back, refusing to jolt like a guilty teenager. They had nothing to be ashamed of.

"We, uh, saw the news and decided to drive on back from Mobile." Her father didn't seem to know where to look.

The news. Right.

At some point in the past ten days, Abbey really should have sent an email or *something* giving them a heads up about what was going on.

Taking Kyle's hand in hers, she offered a nervous smile. "I can explain."

CHAPTER 14

*E*xplain? Kyle struggled not to gawk himself. What exactly was she going to explain?

How he was only here because of an accidental fake engagement? How they were really together despite that? How his very presence had drawn back one of the people who'd nearly ruined their lives and livelihood?

She'd said she'd told no one about their near elopement all those years ago. Did that include her parents? If not, what had they thought of his silence and distance all these years? Had they thought he'd thrown away and abandoned the gift of family, too?

"So... um... engaged?" Faye asked carefully, gaze automatically going to the ring on Abbey's left hand.

How had they not gotten around to discussing what they were going to tell her parents?

"It's complicated."

Kyle wanted to laugh, though there was nothing funny about the situation. Was there any version of this that didn't make them look insane? He should probably say... something. But what? He'd been out of their lives for even longer than he'd been out of Abbey's. Best to let her take the lead.

"Kyle's been here helping me with Granddaddy."

Really? She was starting with that?

Mark frowned. "When you told us you'd lined up help, I never imagined... this."

Kyle's mind filled that hesitation with a multitude of other descriptors. None of them good or flattering. Good Lord. Did Mark think Abbey had shipped them off so that she could sneak him back onto the farm for… Yeah, Kyle couldn't even allow himself to consider that one or he'd start worrying Mark would grab the nearest shotgun.

Abbey laughed, but there was a faint edge to it. "Oh no. He wasn't part of the plan. But there was a… miscommunication on an interview, where the host announced we were engaged. Kyle came home to tell me and…"

"One thing led to another?" Faye suggested.

As his brain conjured flashes of bare skin and ragged breaths, Kyle wished the floor would just open up and swallow him.

"We had a long overdue clearing of the air. And he stayed."

Kyle tensed, waiting for their disapproval and outrage. He deserved it. But they only stood where they were, looking confused.

"And you got actually engaged?" Mark asked.

"No. We put on a show for the paparazzi. But we are together." As if she sensed his need for reassurance, Abbey squeezed his hand.

Faye closed her eyes, and the bottom dropped out of Kyle's stomach. This was it. The incredulity and recriminations for dragging Abbey into all this. The disbelief that they'd be so foolish. The what the actual hell are y'all thinking?

When she opened her eyes again, they shone with tears, and he felt about two feet tall.

"Oh, thank God."

Huh?

Before Kyle could process her words, Faye rushed across the room to pull him into a firm, gardenia-scented hug. "Welcome home, honey."

The unrestrained warmth in her tone and the fierceness with which she hung on stunned and humbled him. And the little boy he'd been, who'd idolized her and endured the mom hugs and discipline with equal parts squirming discomfort and yearning, wrapped his arms around her, burying his face in her hair. His voice cracked when he murmured, "Missed you." And, God, he had. More than he'd let himself think about for years.

Mark was waiting when she finally let him go. He was less effusive, but his handshake was just as warm. "About time."

Kyle wasn't sure if he meant the coming home or being with Abbey, and he wasn't about to ask. He was too busy reeling at this unexpected and unquestioning welcome back into the fold.

"Thank you." His hand found Abbey's again, needing her as an anchor. "I'm afraid it's not all good news."

Faye's face froze. "Roy?"

"No, no. Granddaddy's fine," Abbey assured them. "He sprained his ankle the day you left for your trip, but he's already bouncing back."

"Then what?" Mark asked.

"Maybe we should all sit down." Abbey led

by example, tugging him down onto the sofa beside her.

Her parents found their own seats, and Kyle tried to find the words. Might as well rip the Band-Aid off. "My mother is out of prison. She showed up here this morning."

Faye's eyes, so like Abbey's, went fierce. "She can't have you."

The thickening in Kyle's throat kept him from answering immediately. With another squeeze of his hand, Abbey stepped in.

"That's not what she's about. Never has been. She's trying to blackmail Kyle, threatening to go to the press about everything that happened if he doesn't pay her."

Mark frowned, leaning forward. "What does she think that's gonna do? The evidence was iron clad."

"There's no telling what version of the story she'd spin up. Not one resembling the truth beyond one salient point—that my testimony sent them to prison. I know she'll concoct some kind of story that makes them look like the victims. And, yeah, the actual evidence is clear-cut, but the gossip rags won't care about that. They care about what sells. Scandal—even old scandal—sells. My entire reputation is as the good guy, the nice guy, who never does anything wrong."

"You didn't. You found out what was happening and turned them in. That's the right thing. The hard thing. And you were only a child," Faye insisted.

"You know that, and I know that. But the media isn't likely to dig deep enough for it to matter." Dropping his head, Kyle sucked in a bracing breath. "She's going to keep coming. Going to keep pressing. I wouldn't put it past her to try to do something to upset all of you because you matter to me, and she's always resented that I chose you over them. The only answer, as I can see, is to tell the story first. The problem with that is that it's going to stir everything back up again, and because of the celebrity I've earned, y'all are bound to have to deal with the press all over again."

"Then we deal with the press." Mark shrugged. "We have nothing to hide, and we've got no compunction sharing the absolute truth. Your testimony saved our family business."

"You have our support in this. You always have," Faye assured him. "So do what you need to do."

They meant it.

Kyle didn't understand it. Didn't feel as if he deserved it, but he recognized the gift as what it was.

He'd do anything to protect this. Anything to protect them. If that meant baring his most deeply held secrets—so be it.

As long as he had Abbey to come home to in the end, nothing else mattered. And as he took in her soft smile, he thought about what Granddaddy had said before his mother showed up and ruined the morning. Maybe the old man was right, and he'd waited long enough.

"You two have been manning the ship for nearly two weeks. Go take some time for yourselves," Faye urged. "Have fun."

Abbey hardly knew what to do with herself not having to think about Granddaddy. Kyle had other ideas. "Let's go take a walk in the orchard. I'm feeling nostalgic, and with everything going on, I haven't had the chance to do that since I came home."

Abbey's heart warmed at hearing him slide back into calling this home. Was he aware of it? She let it ride as he took her hand and tugged her toward the trees. There was too much to think about and process. At the end of the day, her parents were supportive, and despite the threat from Twyla, she was feeling good about where she and Kyle stood. Maybe with their immediate responsibilities relieved, they'd have a chance to think about them and where they wanted to go next.

His long, strong fingers felt so good

wrapped around hers, like a puzzle piece snapping into place.

"I used to wish you'd do this when we were younger."

"Do what?"

"Hold my hand."

Kyle glanced over in surprise. "Really?"

"I don't know when holding hands with you started to mean something more. Obviously we did it all the time when we were little. But later… I used to angst about it, wonder if I could sort of nudge you into it without it being weird."

His laugh rolled out. "Nudging isn't your way. You're bold, saying exactly what you think, regardless of consequences. I always loved that about you. That fearlessness was so damned appealing. I always wished it would rub off on me."

Abbey rolled her eyes. "You're plenty fearless. You perform in front of thousands of people. I can't even squeak in front of anyone but you."

"That's different. You're brave in everyday ways."

"I don't know that it's bravery so much as lack of patience for talking around things. The world would run smoother if more people said what they think instead of beating around the bush."

"Probably." He swung their hands in a wide arc. "Know what I think?"

"What?"

"That I'm glad to finally have some time alone with you." The teasing promise in his tone had her blood heating.

"Why, Kyle Keenan, do you have plans out in this orchard?"

"As a matter of fact, I do."

Abbey hoped they were naked plans. She'd had her share of those fantasies over the years as they'd gotten older. Although, with the sun going down, it would get a little cold for that. Still, a girl could dream.

He led her down the rows, way out to the back, far, far from the house. She knew his destination before he cut across the neat lanes toward the oldest trees in the orchard.

Their tree. He was taking her to their tree.

Nothing in his easy gait gave anything away, but Abbey's heart began to pound nonetheless. It didn't necessarily mean anything. This place was important to them for lots of reasons. But as they approached, lights winked on, and she gasped.

Fairy lights were woven throughout the boughs, casting a magical glow over the blanket spread out beneath. A fat picnic basket sat in one corner.

He held up his hand with a tiny remote. "Surprise."

She thought of the story he'd spun for their interview, about how he'd proposed the second time. Was this...? "Kyle?"

His lips curved in a secret smile as he drew her in, close enough to curve a hand around her waist. "Because of how everything went down, I never got to give you the romance you deserve. Let me give you tonight."

She'd give him forever, if only he'd ask. But she only nodded and let him lead her to the blanket.

"Hungry?"

How could she be hungry when he'd done all this? She hummed a noncommittal note he apparently took as a yes.

"We've got fried chicken from the diner and some of Crystal's mac and cheese. Pie, too, although that wasn't my first choice of dessert." His heated, impish look told Abbey he'd meant her.

So maybe this was a seduction, not a proposal? She could absolutely get behind that. Still, he had to know where her mind was going with this. If she was going to relax enough to enjoy what he'd created, she was going to need a confirmation of expectation so her brain didn't keep spinning. "Kyle?"

He lifted his head from the basket. "Hm?"

"Is this just about romancing me or is it something else?"

His mouth opened, then closed again on a

huff of a laugh. One hand scooped through his hair. "I had a plan. I was going to ply you with champagne and good food, then make love to you while the stars came out. And when you were limp and sated, I was going to do what I didn't have the chance at ten years ago."

Heart thrumming, Abbey could barely breathe, but she forced out her words. "And that is?"

Kyle shifted onto one knee, reaching into his pocket to bring out the bubble gum ring.

"Oh my God." She covered her mouth, as much to hold in a scream as a squee.

"You're in it now, Abs," he warned. "We're officially reversing the order of the evening." He reached to take her hand, and his trembled faintly. "I love you. I've loved you since we were practically in diapers. The last time I did this, I told instead of asking. This time I want to do it right—or as close to right as I can get, since you're already wearing my ring. You can choose that one or this one, or we can find something entirely new. You can have whatever you want. But I need to know, Abbey Rhodes Whittaker, if you'll marry me for real. If you'll build a life with me. A home with me. What do you say?"

She'd given up on this dream a long, long time ago. Yet here he knelt, ring in hand, heart on his sleeve, offering the promise and the life they'd both wanted for twenty-five years. In answer, she launched herself at him, catching him around the shoulders and bowling him backward until she sprawled atop him, and he was laughing.

"Is that a yes?"

"Yes." She pressed a kiss to his mouth. "Yes, to all of it." His cheeks. "Also, yes to reversing the order of your plan."

Those beloved blue eyes went dark. "I can get behind that."

She lowered her lips to his again, her fingers already skating beneath his shirt to find warm skin beneath. They rolled, hands touching, taking as they shed layer after layer, until they were naked, and she rose over him.

His eyes were molten as he gripped her hips. "Mine. My Abbey."

"Mine," she agreed, and sank down, taking him into her body.

They both groaned as he filled and stretched her. Bending low, she captured his mouth and began to move. And beneath the branches of the old apple tree where she'd first said yes, she rode him until they both shouted yes again as they shot over the edge.

A long time later, she roused herself to reach for the picnic basket. "I'm starving."

"I will endeavor to keep you fed for the rest of our lives." It was a lazy promise, but Abbey couldn't help but think about the future.

Container of chicken in hand, she came back to kiss him. "I like the sound of that. How does Monday sound?"

"For what?"

"To start the rest of our lives."

Kyle blinked at her and sat up on one elbow. "You want to get married on Monday?"

She wanted to get married right now, to

seal the deal so life didn't have a chance to intervene. But Monday was as early as they could get a license. "Yes."

"You still want to elope?"

How could she explain the depth of her fear that this would get taken away from her again? She didn't want a chance for either of them to think or second guess. She just wanted to be his wife. "Yeah. The end result has always been a lot more important to me than the pomp and circumstance."

His eyes searched hers. Abbey hoped the faint tinge of panic didn't show. At last, he took her ring hand and pressed a kiss to her knuckles.

"As you wish."

CHAPTER 15

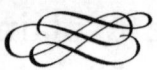

From the front passenger seat of his Land Cruiser, Kyle studied his brother with amusement. "Why the hell are you so twitchy? I'm the one getting married."

Griff grunted, his eyes making the circuit of side mirror to rear view to straight ahead for what felt like the nine-thousandth time. "We should have gone to Knoxville."

"There wasn't time to get to Knoxville and back before our one o'clock appointment with the judge. Hell, even making it to Johnson City and back is pushing it, but by damn, I'm marrying Abbey in a tux and bringing her a dress. I know she said she didn't care, but I don't want her to look back on our wedding day and regret it isn't more special."

"That's sweet and all, but Johnson City is the closest town of any size. Which means any paparazzi hanging around are probably staying there. I don't like it."

"That's what you're for, my brother. Besides, it's a quick in and out. Easy peasy. No one knows I'm getting married, let alone that I'm going to be in Johnson City."

Griff just grunted again.

It would be fine. They'd grab the proper wedding day attire and meet Abbey and Granddaddy at the courthouse. It'd be cutting it close, but the look on her face at his surprise would be worth it. Kyle wasn't at all sure how her parents would react to being excluded. She'd originally intended to have a single witness, but Kyle knew how important it was to Granddaddy to be a part of things, and it hadn't taken much to convince her to bring him along. He didn't exactly like the haste she was pushing for, but he understood it for what it was. Even knowing they'd both been played ten years ago, she was afraid of a repeat.

Over his dead body. He was marrying that girl, come hell or high water. Maybe they'd have a big party for family and friends when everything was done. Once she accepted he wasn't going anywhere, she'd want to celebrate.

Despite Griff's dire predictions, they made it to the bridal shop without incident. After a snoop through Abbey's closet to check, Kyle had already called this morning with his measurements and Abbey's height and size. The proprietress had promised to have a selection of dresses available on their arrival.

He flashed the Nice Guy grin at the fifty-something woman behind the counter. "Order for Griffin Powell?"

Griff arched a brow, but Kyle just shrugged. Using his own name hadn't been an option.

"Oh, of course. I have the tux right here, if you'd like to try it on."

"I'd really like to see the dresses first." One monkey suit was more or less like another, in his opinion. The dress was more important.

"Certainly. Right this way."

Kyle trailed her through a curtain into a massive dressing room. Multiple stalls circled the space, and a small, raised dais occupied the center of the room in front of a three-way mirror. A single dress hung on the hook outside of each dressing room. Looked like they had the place to themselves for the moment.

"Based on what you told me, I pulled about half a dozen gowns. These styles will be the most forgiving if your estimates are off." She moved from one dress to the next, listing features that meant next to nothing to him.

The last dress had some kind of design on the bodice that reminded Kyle of the spreading branches of an apple tree. It was a sign. "That one."

"Oh, an excellent choice. A-line with a Vneck is flattering on a multitude of body types."

Kyle didn't much care what kind of alphabet soup features it had. He just knew Abbey would be stunning in it. "Wrap it up."

"Certainly. And you should try on your tux while I do that."

"I'm sure it's fine."

"I'm afraid I must insist. You don't want to get to the wedding, and it not fit properly."

Though he knew time was running short, he did as he was told. Maybe he'd just wear it back to the Ridge and save time.

Several minutes later, he stepped out into the main shop, looking for Griff. "Well?" Arms held out, he spun a slow circle.

But his brother was looking through a doorway on the other side of the counter, his granite jaw bunching and flexing.

"What is it?"

"A problem."

Kyle crossed over and peered in himself,

spotting a TV playing on low volume. His name flashed on the screen.

Kyle Keenan's Estranged Mother Tells All!

The blood drained from his face. "No." Even as he uttered the word, Twyla filled the screen.

He'd circled around the counter and barged into the office to raise the volume, despite the objection from the saleswoman.

"—been hard. But I want my boy to know, I forgive him. I only wish I could be there for his wedding today to tell him."

His blood ran cold. "How? How did she know?"

"Question for later. We need to move." Urgency thrummed in Griff's tone. He disappeared from the office doorway, and the shop owner popped in.

"Sir, you can't just..." She trailed off, looking from Kyle to where his face was now splashed on the screen. Her eyes went wide. "You're... oh my."

"Look, I'll take the tux and the dress." Kyle

pulled cash out of his wallet. "And your silence. I don't want any trouble. I just want to get married today."

Her expression softened. She took the money, counted out a stack and gave back the rest. "No one will hear it from me."

"Thank you."

Griff came back, Kyle's clothes in hand. "Wear the tux. We need to go before anybody finds you."

The proprietress handed him the garment bag with the dress. Kyle draped it over one arm. "Need my phone. I have to call and warn Abbey."

Griff slapped it into his hand. "Talk and move."

He could wait 'til they got in the truck.

They burst out of the shop, and chaos descended. Cameras flashed; people shouted. Bodies pressed in close.

"Is it true you sent your parents to prison?"

Panic and temper surged, but he knew better than to let either fly. No comment was

the party line until his team told him otherwise. The team he hadn't yet talked to.
Damn it.

Griff put himself between Kyle and the
throngs. But he was only one man.

"Were you part of the embezzlement
scheme?"

Someone shoved a camera in Kyle's face.

"Did you make sure your parents took the
fall?"

Someone jostled Kyle, and his phone went
flying. The paparazzi surged forward, and the
crunch of glass told him the phone was a lost
cause.

"Fuck this," Griff snarled. "Stay close." He
bulled his way through the crowd, much as
he'd done as a defensive lineman in high
school football. They broke through and
bolted for the Land Cruiser. Press swarmed
the SUV before they'd even gotten inside.
They slammed their doors, nearly mashing a
few fingers.

"Hold on to your butt." Griff gunned it, and

reporters scattered, leaping out of the way as the Toyota bumped over a curb and shot away from the parking lot.

"Shit. Shit. Shit" This couldn't be happening. Not today, of all days.

"They're right on our tail."

Kyle curled his hand around the oh shit handle. "Can you lose them?"

"Yeah, but you're gonna be late. There's only one way to Eden's Ridge from here, and we can't take it."

"Shit. I need to warn Abbey. Where's your phone?"

"Pocket. Where's yours?"

"Toast. Dropped it back at the shop."

They careened around a corner before Griff dug his out and tossed it over.

Kyle stared at the thing in his hand. "What the hell is this?"

"A phone."

"It's a flip phone."

"So?"

Now was not the time to give his brother

shit for not being part of the twenty-first century. "Fine." He flipped it open only to come
up short. "I don't know her number."

"Seriously?"

"Why would I? It's a button in my contacts.
Smartphones mean we never have to actually
dial anything."

"Well, I don't have it."

"I'll call the inn. One of my sisters will
have it."

"Don't have that one either."

And because it was a technological antique,
Kyle couldn't just look it up. "Well, who do
you have?"

"You, a few other guys on the crew. Some
friends from the Marines."

"That's it?

"In case it escaped your notice, I haven't
exactly been out making friends since I got
out of the Corps. I've been babysitting your
ass."

Kyle slammed his hand against the dash.
"Fuck! If I don't show, Abbey's going to think

I bailed on her." He couldn't do that to her. Not again. Not as scared as she was of exactly that.

"Would you rather lead these cretins, straight to her?"

He thought of the overzealous press, imagined them mobbing her at the courthouse. Yeah, he didn't want that as a memory on their wedding day either. "No."

"Then you'll explain later. I'll back you up, and she'll forgive you. Right now, my job is to keep you safe. But this situation is bigger than us. You need PR. So I'm taking you to your people."

"What?"

"We're going to Nashville."

As the clock ticked closer to one, Abbey paced the third-floor hall outside the judge's chambers. "Where is he?"

"Settle down, Butter Bean. He'll be here."

Granddaddy's assurances did nothing to quell the anxiety curdling her stomach.

"I don't understand why we didn't come together." So she could have kept an eye on her groom. Not that she didn't trust him. Kyle loved her. She knew that. But despite understanding that they'd both been played ten years ago, she couldn't shake the fear or the memories of devastation. She needed him here with her.

"He's working on a surprise for you."

Cluing in to the conspiratorial tone, Abbey zeroed in on her grandfather. "What do you know, old man?"

"I'm sworn to secrecy. But I promise, it'll be worth the wait." The twinkle in his eyes helped her relax enough to sit beside him. He folded her hand between both of his. "Are you sure you wanna do it like this? No family but me?"

"Yes." She'd meant what she'd told Kyle. The end result mattered more to her than the wedding itself. "Are you disappointed?" Her parents would be, but she'd deal with them later. After the I dos were said and this nagging sense of disquiet had settled.

"It's not what I imagined for you, but it's not my wedding."

Abbey appreciated that he wasn't laying on the guilt trip. He could have. "What did you imagine?"

"I always thought you'd get married in the orchard. That we'd string up fairy lights and ribbon and make a long aisle down the east side. You'd have flowers in your hair and maybe wear your grandma's veil."

The picture he painted made her throat ache. Under other circumstances, she'd want exactly that. With friends and family there as witness to those vows of forever. Swallowing hard, she tipped her head to his shoulder. "That all sounds lovely. And you'd walk me down the aisle."

"Not your daddy?"

"I always wanted you." Who else but her favorite person?

Granddaddy's wrinkled cheeks pinked with pleasure. "Well, at least we've got that. And this." He reached down to pick up a flat box he'd brought and handed it over.

Curious, Abbey lifted the lid to find a neat pile of gauzy white lace. With trembling hands, she drew it out. "Grandma's veil?"

"I thought it could be your something old."

Touched, delighted, she smoothed the lace. "It's perfect." With careful hands, she fit the comb into her hair, trailing the veil down her back. "How do I look?"

"Beautiful."

The door to the judge's chambers opened. "Miss Whittaker and Mr. Keenan?"

Oh God, it was time, and Kyle wasn't here. Panic flattered in Abbey's gut. "I'm so sorry. The groom is running a little late."

Judge Halsey checked his watch. "Well, we can wait a little bit, but I've got court at two."

"Yes, sir. Thank you." As soon as he disappeared into his office, Abbey was yanking out her phone. "I'm calling him."

But Kyle didn't answer. The tone rang and rang. When it clicked to voicemail, she hissed, "Where are you? The judge is waiting. I'm waiting. And I'm getting worried." Without looking at Granddaddy, she followed up with a text. But the message didn't flip to read and there were no bouncing dots to indicate a reply. Something was *wrong.*

"Okay, seriously, I don't care if he swore you to secrecy. You have to tell me where he went."

Granddaddy sighed. "He wanted today to be special for you, so he went to..." At the sound of hurried footsteps, he trailed off. "See there? I told you he'd be here."

But it wasn't Kyle. The creepy paparazzo from the spa that first day trotted down the hall, his camera bouncing on the strap around his neck.

Abbey's hands curled into fists. "How dare you show up here? Have you no shame? This is our wedding!"

The guy held up a hand as he struggled to catch his breath. "Not gonna... be... a wedding."

Abbey's mouth went dry. "Excuse me?"

"The groom's headed back to Nashville."

"That's ridiculous." Why would this asshat have any idea where Kyle actually was? Except that he'd made it his mission to track everywhere Kyle went.

"Lit out of Johnson City like his ass was on fire once the news broke."

A cold finger of dread trailed its way down her spine. "News? What news?"

"His mama's interview. Everybody else went chasing after him. I was a lot more interested in getting your reaction to being jilted at the altar."

The words slammed into her. She wanted to deny it. To believe Kyle would never do that to her. But he'd called his mom's bluff. If she'd already acted—and how would this guy know anything about Twyla if she hadn't?—he'd panic. What had she said? How bad was it? And why the hell hadn't he called her?

If this was just about damage control or even some kind of necessary postponement of things, he'd have called her. The only reason he'd avoid her calls and not respond to text was if he'd let Twyla and her bullshit into his head. If he believed what she'd been telling him for years. That he was worthless. That he didn't deserve Abbey. That she was better off without him.

"No." As the horror of it slid into her like a blade, a camera flashed in her face. Abbey raised a hand to shield her eyes, her face, from the onslaught.

Granddaddy swore and shouted, "Security!"

Footsteps pounded down the hall. Someone dragged the guy away, but Abbey barely noticed. She was too busy clinging to control by her fingernails.

"After everything we've been through, how could he leave me at the altar? He knows what this means to me. How could he just run back to Nashville without a word?" Her voice cracked as her throat simply closed up with a knot of tears.

"Do you really believe that's what he did, or are you just panicking?"

"Of *course,* I'm panicking. My groom is MIA!" The knot dissolved, and the tears spilled down her cheeks in a hot flood.

"Seems to be the case. But there's more than one potential explanation for that. Maybe he forgot his phone somewhere. I do it all the damned time."

Abbey blinked back tears and looked into Granddaddy's patient face. Could it really be that simple and benign?

Sucking in a breath, she pulled out her phone and did a quick search of Kyle's name. And there was Twyla, in all her hateful glory, along with an inset of video someone had taken in a parking lot. She clicked play and watched as Griff and Kyle straight up bolted to their SUV, diving in as if it were bullets rather than accusations flying. Kyle wore a tux and had a garment bag over one arm.

"What is that?"

"A wedding dress. He wanted to surprise you."

The fist around her heart loosened a fraction. "He… went to buy me a wedding dress?"

"He wanted to make today special for you."

He'd bought her a dress. He was *wearing* a freaking tux when he escaped. None of that said he was calling off the wedding. The panic began to ebb. They wouldn't make their appointment today. Abbey had no clue what the hell was going on or why he'd gone back to Nashville without a word. But he had a reason. She had to trust him like she didn't before. Trust that he loved her, and he'd explain when he had the chance.

Rising, she held out a hand to Granddaddy. "Come on."

"Where are we going?"

"To find him."

CHAPTER 16

"In breaking news, country music's Captain America, Kyle Keenan is looking a lot less Steve Rogers. Allegations from his estranged mother suggest that he lied to send his parents to prison. When confronted by the press, Keenan ran, leaving his intended bride at the altar for their surprise courthouse wedding."

Kyle banged his head back against the seat. "Fuuuuuck!"

Four hours. Abbey had had four hours to think this was the truth. And it sounded like, despite their attempt to lure all the paparazzi away, some had found her at the courthouse, anyway. What was she thinking? What was she feeling? Did she really believe he'd betrayed her? After what happened before, he wouldn't blame her.

Griff switched off the radio. "You don't need to keep listening to this shit."

"I've got to do *something*. Abbey's got to be going out of her mind." Or maybe she was deciding he was more trouble than he was worth, and she was better off without him.

"Deanna will know what to do. Where is her office?"

"Is it safe to even go there?"

"We lost the last tail on that interchange at Briley Parkway."

Kyle had been positive he'd roll the Land Cruiser in the process, but he kept that to himself. "She might not even be there."

"Then hopefully someone else will be and will give you her number."

Kyle gave him directions to the boutique

PR firm. They made it across town without further incident, and Griff hustled him inside.

A security guard rose at their entrance. "Can I help you?"

"Kyle Keenan for Deanna James," Griff barked, scanning all the nooks and crannies of the lobby as if ninjas with cameras would jump out at any moment.

The guy gave Kyle a look that said he'd heard the news, but he reached for the phone and called up. "Kyle Keenan is here to see you, Miss James."

The shouted, "Send him up!" told him she was well aware of the situation and was losing her shit. Not a good sign. Deanna James was one of the most level-headed individuals Kyle knew.

Eyes wide, the guard gently replaced the handset in the cradle, as if that would keep from riling her any further. "Um... you can go up."

The moment the elevator doors opened, Deanna latched onto his arm and dragged him off. "Where the hell have you been? Why haven't you been answering your phone? This is a fucking shit show."

"Phone broke in a scuffle with the paparazzi. Have you heard from Abbey?"

"No. Not that I expect she'd take a call from me if I tried right now. Come on. If we're going to save your reputation, we've got to hurry." Without waiting for a response, she hustled down the hall, high heels clicking on the tile.

That suggested there was a chance, which was more than he'd expected.

In the conference room, she snapped, "Sit."

Kyle sat, noticing the older man at the other end of the table. Silver-white hair waved back from a craggy face that seemed vaguely familiar. One of the senior partners in the firm here for damage control? Or to decide whether they were going to cut him loose?

Deanna pressed her hands to the table, eyes flashing. "There's no point in my berating you for all the things you should have done, so here's where I tell you what you're going to do."

"If you're going to tell me to sign the new contracts with Quicksilver for the protection of their brand, I'd rather walk away right now than go back to that life. My reputation may be trashed beyond repair, but I'd rather lose it all than give up Abbey. If she'll even speak to me after today." Kyle hadn't fully realized that was in his head until it came out of his mouth, but he didn't want to take it back.

Deanna stared at him. "You'd walk away from everything for her?"

"In a heartbeat."

A flash of something that might've been pain crossed her features before her face blanked again. "They broke the mold when they made you." She exchanged a look with the older dude. "Told you."

The leather chair creaked as he leaned back. "That'd be a damned shame. You're a gifted musician, with a lot to offer."

"Not at the expense of the woman I love."

314 | KAIT NOLAN

The guy smiled, and that sense of the familiar grew more pronounced at the sight of that lopsided grin behind the silver beard. "Can't say as I blame you. I like Abbey, and she's very proud of you."

Kyle tensed. "I'm sorry. Who the hell are you?"

"I'm your option for a different kind of life." He offered a hand. "Harry Cafferty."

Kyle's mouth dropped open.

Harry Cafferty was a Nashville legend. A former singer/songwriter himself, he'd made a massive name for himself through the eighties and nineties. Everybody knew he'd been cherry picking talent for his new label. And he was interested in Kyle? But that wasn't the most pressing question.

"You know Abbey?"

"Met her at Jam Night in Eden's Ridge. I was staying at the inn. Caught your new song. I really dig the new direction, and I'd like to give you space at my label. It's smaller and new but it won't require the same tour commitments you've had up to now. I think we'd be a good fit. I was going to go through your manager, but I understand you're between representatives at the moment. When today's... unpleasantness hit, I contacted Deanna. I think I can help."

"With respect, sir, I don't see how the offer of a contract is going to fix this. Not that I'm not honored by the opportunity."

"I've got a showcase of my new artists tonight. I'd love you to join it."

"Even with the publicity nightmare?"

"It's only a nightmare because you haven't faced it. In the absence of an explanation from you, the press and public are free to make up whatever they want. The showcase will be a platform for you to take a stand and make a statement about the situation in a calm and rational way. And the focus will get pulled back to where it needs to be—on your music. You signing with me will help redirect things." Harry flashed that crooked grin again. "I'm kind of a big deal."

Kyle couldn't quite believe this chance was falling into his lap. "Why would you do this for me? It seems like you're the one taking all the risk."

"Because I like your music. Because you remind me of me, and if I'd had more of that heart at your age, I'd still be married."

Deanna arched a brow. "I didn't know you'd been married."

"It was a happened in Vegas thing. Didn't last. Anyway, back to Kyle. Unlike the press, I took the time to look into the actual court case against your parents. They'd have been convicted without your testimony. The addition of it was just the neat bow on top. It might take a bit for that to trickle through, but in the end, it'll all come out in the wash, and your mom's interview will be just a flash in the pan."

Abbey had said more or less the same thing. That the music would ultimately win out. Were they right?

"Do you think it'll work?"

Deanna folded her arms. "It'll do a hell of a lot. I'm no agent, but given what you've said the past few months, this seems like the perfect deal for you."

"Do I have to sign right now to be part of the showcase?"

"We can consider the showcase a handshake agreement, pending a review of the contracts by you and your attorney, with the option to walk away if the terms don't suit."

Kyle couldn't ask for more than that. "What do I need to do?"

As a team, they went over the details and the best way to handle the showcase. Deanna crafted a statement. Harry had several suggestions. Griff asked all the pertinent questions about security. They were all on his side, and by the time they solidified the plan, Kyle felt far less panicked.

"If you're gonna make it to the venue on time, you've gotta hoof it." Deanna made a shooing motion. "Get moving, Keenan."

"Abbey—"

"I'll try to reach her to let her know where you'll be. Get to the showcase. Sort out your love life later."

He'd just have to live with that for now and have faith that Abbey would trust him.

Trailing Griff, he headed downstairs and out to the parking lot.

The paparazzi swarmed the moment they passed the corner of the building. Of course they'd tracked him down here. Kyle's first instinct, as always, was to run. But he remembered what Harry had said—that his silence was just an opportunity for more lies to proliferate. He had to face this head on.

Stopping, he pivoted toward the crowd of cameras and microphones, trying not to flinch at the barrage of flashes.

"I'd like to make a statement."

THE SIDEWALKS outside Kyle's loft were swarming with people. Press. Fans. Paparazzi.

Abbey didn't know. But there was no getting near the place either way. She didn't really think he'd be there. He still wasn't answering the phone, so she'd given up on calling. If Kyle went to ground to hide from all this insanity, where would he go? She'd never been more aware of how much she hadn't been a part of his life as she tried to find him in a city of three-quarters of a million people. And she couldn't call anybody to ask for suggestions because her phone had died on the drive, and there was no charger in her car. Of course.

Leaving the crowd around the loft in her rearview, Abbey clenched the steering wheel until her knuckles went white. "I don't know where else to look."

"Buck up, Butter Bean. Think. Do you know any more of Joan's kids who live in Nashville? Maybe one of them has heard from him."

"I don't... Wait. Caleb. He and his wife are in Hamilton, just outside the city proper. I saw them at the last family reunion. He and Kyle are still tight, even after all these years. I wasn't at the wedding, but I sent a gift. Pin Oak Drive. I don't remember the house number, but I'd recognize his truck."

Of course, that was assuming Caleb wasn't on duty at the fire station or that his house didn't have a garage door. Abbey wasn't above going door to door to ask, just to have something active to do.

Thankfully, it didn't come to that. Caleb's big truck was parked in the driveway, exactly as she'd hoped. As soon as she'd parked, Abbey scrambled out, helping Granddaddy up the walk. Sucking in a breath that did nothing to calm her racing heart, she rang the bell.

An unfamiliar teenager answered the door, and Abbey hesitated. Did she have the wrong house, after all?

"Can I help you?"

"I'm looking for Caleb Romero."

"Oh, sure. He's here." She called over her shoulder. "Caleb! People here for you!"

A brown-and-white pit bull mix nosed

around the girl, tail wagging, before Caleb himself filled the doorway. "Abbey?'"

At the sight of a familiar face, her knees went weak. "Is Kyle here?"

Brows pulling together in concern, Caleb shook his head. "No. What's going on?"

Tears of frustration formed a knot in her throat. This had been her only idea. If he wasn't here, then where the hell was he?

Caleb pulled her in for a hug. "Hey. What-ever it is, it'll be okay."

Abbey hiccupped and squeezed him in gratitude. Since she'd removed herself from Kyle's life, Caleb was probably his closest friend. He'd help her figure this out.

"Come on in, both of you."

Caleb ushered them into the living room. "You remember my wife, Emerson. And that's her daughter, Fiona, who met you at the door. And this is Abbey's grandfather, Roy Whittaker."

"Good memory."

"It's been a minute since I had that summer

job in the orchards, but I never forget a friendly face."

Abbey tried to stem the tears that wanted to flow as she lifted a hand to wave at the brunette perched in one of the chairs. "Hi. Sorry to barge in like this."

Emerson hefted herself out of the chair, leading with her pregnant belly. "Nonsense. I don't know what's going on, but I can tell by the look on your face, it calls for tea. I'll go make some."

"Oh, don't go to any trouble on my account."

"It's no trouble." Emerson squeezed Abbey's arm and strode into the kitchen.

"Go on and sit down," Caleb ordered.

Abbey dropped onto one end of the sofa, wrapping both arms around her middle. "Have you talked to Kyle?"

"Not for a couple of weeks. He said he was staying at the farm with you."

"He is. Was. I don't actually know what he's doing right now."

Emerson came back and laid a hand on her shoulder. "Why don't you start at the beginning?"

Granddaddy eased down onto the sofa himself. "No time for that. A summary will have to do. Kyle accidentally said he was engaged to Abbey in a TV interview and finally came home to warn her. I convinced him to convince her to fake it for the press, figuring that would finally make them talk and clear the air, which it did. They got engaged for real and were getting married this afternoon, but his mama opened up some can of lies, and he got mobbed by paparazzi while picking up his tux and up and disappeared with Griff. Now we can't raise him on the phone, the press thinks he jilted my girl at the altar, and we've gotta find him."

They all stared at him until Abbey waved a hand in his direction. "Basically, all that."

"Wow. That's... a lot. Maybe she needs whiskey instead," Fiona suggested.

"That's Kyle's drink. After his mom's interview I wouldn't be surprised if he's indulging, but I don't know *where*."

Caleb leaned forward, bracing his elbows on his knees. "Wait, his mom's out of prison?"

"Yeah. Straight to causing him trouble. You know how she treats him, how she can push his buttons. I have to talk to him. Do you have any idea where he'd go?"

He rubbed a hand on the back of his neck. "If not here or home, I doubt he's out in public anywhere. After everything that happened with the trial, he hates the press."

"Have you checked the gossip blogs?" Fiona asked. "If the paparazzi are tailing him, it might give us some clue where he's been or where he's going."

"I haven't checked anything. My phone died a couple hours ago."

Fiona retrieved a laptop and joined her on the couch. "There's this one that has a community component. People can post about celebrity sightings, and it shows up on a map with a date and time stamp."

"That's creepy and invasive as hell."

Fiona's fingers flew over the keyboard. "But helpful in this case. He's been all over Nashville." She shifted the screen so Abbey could see. The dotted line on the map did indeed criss-cross the city.

"What are these little icons?"

"Pictures and video." Scanning the map, she hovered over an entry. "There's a video attached to this most recent one."

Everyone gathered around the sofa as she clicked on the link. The video loaded. It began with Kyle, still in his tux, getting cornered outside an office building. He was still with Griff, thank God. The bigger man was shoving his way through the noisy crowd. Then Kyle stopped and faced the multitude of cameras, face grim. "I'd like to make a statement."

The assembled people quieted down.

"Allegations have been made against me that have prompted folks to question my integrity and my honesty. With no substantiation, I've been accosted by paparazzi at a very sensitive time, putting me in a position where I hurt the person I care the most about." He shifted his gaze from one camera to another, as if searching for something. "I want and deserve the chance to tell my story the right way. If you want to see the future of my career—the future of my everything—come to the Two Lane Records showcase tonight." He named a venue.

Abbey loosed a trembling breath. "He's banking that I see this. That was a message for me. It's where he's going to be. I have to get there."

Caleb straightened. "I know exactly where that is. I'll drive."

CHAPTER 17

Kyle tore his attention away from the artist currently on stage. "Anything?"

Griff shook his head.

It was a long shot that Abbey had gotten his message. Longer still that she could get here if she had seen the statement. Eden's Ridge was four hours away. But he needed to know she was okay. That she'd give him a chance to explain and make up for the shit show of today.

Kyle turned back to the stage, gaze skipping past the female duo currently captivating the audience to scan the faces in the first several rows, as if they'd somehow changed in the past couple of minutes. Harry Cafferty's new label commanded a hell of a crowd. While the styles of music showcased tonight varied widely, the musician in him appreciated that they all shared that indefinable something he thought of as soul. This music all *said* something. It was exactly what he wanted to produce, and he felt like joining Harry's label put him in good company. His gut said it was the right call for his future career.

But he couldn't think about his career right now. Not when he still compulsively scanned the crowd for a familiar blonde head.

"Mr. Keenan, you're up next."

A muscle jumped in his jaw. He didn't want to do this now. Not yet. Not without knowing she was here.

At the flash of blonde hair in his peripheral vision, his heart leapt into his throat. But, of course, it wasn't Abbey. It was Deanna. She wove through the equipment and people backstage, cutting toward him.

Wiping his hands on his pants, he met her halfway. "Did you get ahold of Abbey?"

"I tried, but the calls kept going straight to voicemail. I sent a few texts, told her you'd be here, but she never responded."

It didn't necessarily mean the worst. But Kyle's heart sank nonetheless. She was probably upset. She absolutely had every right to be. But even if she tried to cut him off again, he wouldn't just accept it this time. He'd go back to the Ridge. He'd camp out and make her listen. Just as soon as he could shake loose here.

At the sound of applause, he recognized he couldn't afford to wait anymore.

Showtime.

Grabbing the borrowed guitar, Kyle took a breath and strode out on stage. At the sight of him, the crowd stirred. Yeah, there were people here who'd heard, who wondered. But plenty still cheered and applauded as he took his seat on the lone stool they'd set out for him.

"Good evenin'! I'm Kyle Keenan, and I'm delighted to be a part of Two Lane Records' showcase tonight. But before I introduce you to my music, there are some things I need to say."

He paused, still scanning faces, though the bright lights from the stage kept him from seeing more than vague impressions. "You probably think I'm a bit overdressed for tonight." He'd made the call to keep on the tux, though he'd gotten rid of the tie. "The fact is, I was supposed to get married this afternoon."

A surprised murmur swept through the venue.

"There are rumors flying around that I jilted my fiancée at the altar. The truth is, I was accosted by paparazzi while picking up my tux and her dress. It seems that my es-tranged mother gave an interview alleging... well, a whole boatload of things. People are questioning whether I've been lying all this time. About who I am. What I believe. The kind of man I am."

He hated spilling this out. But he remembered what Abbey had said. That shame was like a shadow. It couldn't exist in the light. It was time to stop hiding from the past.

"I've just been trying to live my life. Be a regular guy. I didn't want people to know where I came from. What I came from. My parents are troubled people, and when I was thirteen, I turned them into the police for embezzlement and drug crimes."

In the silence, Kyle could hear the hum of speakers. He absolutely had their attention, and it didn't feel half as scary being the one to deliberately command it. Not when he was in control.

"I'm not getting into the details of that. The ensuing investigation thoroughly substantiated my accusation, and they both went to prison. I went into foster care. And it was one of the best things to ever happen to me. I got a huge supportive family out of the deal—one I thought I had to distance myself from in order to keep the rest hidden. I'd like to publicly apologize to all of them for that. My brothers and sisters are some of the best people I know, and I've missed the hell out of all of you."

He paused again, gaze sweeping the crowd. But he wasn't really seeing them anymore. He just wanted to take the moment to measure their temperature, give them a second to absorb his words. This was a statement, not an apology, and they'd better get used to it.

"I'm done hiding. I'm done letting the shame of where I came from be the driving force behind my actions. The woman I love has been calling me on that for twenty-five years, and it's long past time for me to acknowledge she's right. I'm not my parents. Their mistakes aren't mine. God knows, I've made plenty of my own. But stopping them from hurting some of the kindest, most hardworking people I've ever known wasn't one of them. So, if all of this means you can no longer think of me as county music's Captain

America, that's fine. I'm just Kyle Keenan. The guy who really hopes he hasn't blown it with the most important person in his life."

He shifted the guitar, fingers slipping into place. "This song was one we wrote together years ago, and I only wish she was here tonight to hear it."

Without giving the audience a moment to react, he began to pick out a melody that had lived in his heart for as long as he could remember.

As THE FIRST notes of the song rang out, Abbey resumed her fight to get to the stage. She could've taken advantage of the absolute silence while Kyle had been talking, but she didn't want to do anything to distract from or minimize the impact of what he'd said. He'd taken control, taken a stand, removing his mom's leverage once and for all. Abbey had never been prouder.

She needed to get to him, but here were so many people in her way, and she kept turning back to check on Granddaddy.

He squeezed her elbow. "Go get him, Butter Bean. I'm fine."

"We've got him," Emerson promised, linking her arm through his. Fiona took the other.

"C'mon. I'll get you up there." Caleb used his broader bulk to clear a path toward the side stage.

Abbey stayed close in his wake as Kyle continued to sing.

They weren't moving fast enough. She wasn't going to make it before he finished.

But then something miraculous happened. People in the crowd began to actually see her. Some recognized her and stepped aside, making room for her to pass. Who ever would have imagined she'd be glad her face had been splashed in gossip magazines and on TV?

A pair of burly guys in black T-shirts

blocked access to the backstage area. Venue security.

"Look, I have to get back there. I'm his fiancée."

"Sure you are, sweet cheeks."

She'd made it too damned far and was too damned close to let a couple of over-grown Neanderthals stop her from getting to Kyle. But before she could do something that would make a scene, Griff appeared at their backs.

"Thank Christ. She's with us. Come on." He tugged her past the guys and up the stairs. "He's been going out of his mind."

"Same. I need a mic."

"You what?"

"I need a mic. Right now."

Deanna fell into step beside them, her brows drawn together. "What are you doing? I thought you don't perform."

She could see Kyle out on that stage, just a couple dozen feet away, and her heart lifted. "I don't. Get me a mic before I lose my nerve."

Somebody put one in her hand and turned it

on. Abbey didn't stop to think, didn't look around, didn't take her eyes off the best friend she was never walking away from again. She began to sing, adding in the harmony as he reached the second chorus. Kyle's head whipped up from his guitar in shock, though he didn't skip a beat. When she strode on stage to join him, it was easier than she'd imagined because, with all the lights, all she could see was him.

Shock and joy spread over his face as he spotted her. And it was worth the noodle knees and pterodactyls swooping in her stomach to be here, surprising him like this. She met him center stage, keeping her focus entirely on him, as his was now on her.

When the last notes died away, they stood there, breathing hard, staring at each other. Kyle finally set the guitar aside and closed the distance between them. His eyes were suspiciously shiny as he cupped her cheeks. "You sang."

"Just to you."

Then he kissed her, and the crowd lost its collective mind. All of it faded as she wrapped around him. Relief and love crashed through her. They'd been derailed but not broken. They'd made it back to each other, and in the end, nothing else mattered.

He eased back, pressing his brow to hers. "I love you."

"Love you, too."

The cheering and whooping finally sank in, and Abbey actually looked at the audience. The stage did a slow dip.

Kyle locked his arm tighter around her. "Nope. No passing out now. You already did the hard part."

She still couldn't quite believe she'd done it. Now that it was over, she really, *really* needed to get away from all these people before she embarrassed herself further by passing out or hurling. Lifting the mic, she addressed the crowd. "I'm sorry, y'all. You're going to have to excuse us. My groom here has a prior engagement, and he's really, really late."

Beneath the renewed cheering and laughter, Kyle murmured, "We're still doing that?"

"Damned straight." As he escorted her off-stage, she said, "Although we seem to be snake-bit when it comes to eloping, so maybe we should do something radical this time and actually plan a wedding. Preacher. Family. The whole shebang."

Kyle brought her hand to his lips. "There's nothing I'd love more."

EPILOGUE

"Hold still," Pru ordered.

Kyle resisted the urge to tell her he could tie his own bowtie. This was part of having family involved in his big day, and he was grateful they were all here.

"There." She smoothed her hands across his shoulders and down the sleeves of his jacket, brushing away imaginary lint. "You clean up pretty well."

"Thanks."

"You nervous?"

"To marry my best friend? No. Easiest

thing I've ever done. Worried she'll wake up one day and realize she made a mistake? I'll probably always have a little of that."

"She loves you. Always has, even during those years you were both being stupid."

"I don't think I'll ever truly feel worthy of that. But I intend to spend the rest of my life making sure she doesn't regret it."

"There are worse approaches to marriage." She fastened on his apple blossom boutonniere. "Will y'all stick around here?"

Kyle curled his hands around her shoulders. "To answer the question you really want to know and are too polite to ask, I'm not taking Abbey away from the spa or the Ridge. She loves it here, and I'm able to write here in a way I haven't been able to in years. I'm sure she'll travel with me some when I do tour, but Harry wants his artists to have lives and families, so they won't be what I had to do before." He'd basically offered Kyle his dream career on a platter. "All that to say, I'm home, sis."

Pru sniffed, her dark eyes shining. "Good. That's good. Where will you live?"

Kyle glanced around the room that no longer bore any resemblance to the childhood bedroom he'd spent as little time in as possible. "Here. For now, anyway. Abbey and I want to be close to Granddaddy. Beyond that, if we want, Mark and Faye have no problem with us adding on for more space." He'd initially rejected the idea of that, but he loved the orchards, and a part of him relished the thought of taking the last shadow of his childhood and reclaiming it in the name of their future. He'd talk to Porter after the wedding and the honeymoon and see what he could draw up.

"Taking control of the last piece. Mom would be proud."

Kyle thought of the woman who, other than Abbey, had given him back the biggest pieces of himself. "I wish Joan could have been here today."

Pru smiled. "She is, if only in all of us."

The idea was a comfort.

"We should get out there. Guests are arriving, and the ceremony starts soon."

Someone knocked on the door.

"Come in."

The door opened, and Abbey slipped inside.

Pru leapt in front of him, arms stretched wide, as if her five-foot-something frame would hide him. "What are you doing here! You can't see the groom before the wedding!"

"I'm not in my dress yet, and we're not the superstitious type. I need to talk to Kyle."

Did Pru hear that note of nerves beneath the easy bravado? If she did, she didn't comment as she vacated the room.

"Fine, but the ceremony is in T-minus less than half an hour. Don't be late."

"Yes, ma'am," Kyle promised.

Then they were alone, and his bride to be bit her berry-glossed lip. Because he knew she had a little trauma where trying to marry him was concerned, Kyle crossed over and took her hands. "Needed to make sure I was here?"

"Maybe partly. Although if you did want to bolt, I think you'd have to get past a hundred or so people to pull it off."

"Not going anywhere without my bride." He stroked his thumbs over the pulse points in her wrists. "What's wrong, Abs?"

Her hair was swept up, her makeup perfect. She was ready but for the fact that she wore a silky white robe declaring her "The Bride." But something was very clearly off. "I needed to ask you something."

"Okay." He'd say or do whatever she needed to be reassured.

"What are you doing in seven months?"

Kyle frowned as he did mental math. "At Christmas? I expect I'll be right here with you enjoying my first family Christmas in a decade."

"We haven't talked about that. The whole family thing. Like whether we want one."

"Is that what you're worried about? That I don't want kids?"

"I mean, it's kind of a big thing couples should be on the same page about."

"I love the idea of having children with you. Of Christmas mornings when we get up way too early after going to bed way too late because we were up putting together whatever ridiculous toys we bought. Of all those everyday things people take for granted. I want to make the family I didn't have growing up."

"Then you won't mind if we get started on that early?"

Kyle tightened his hands on hers. "You want to start trying for a baby at Christmas?"

"Yeah, about that." Abbey swallowed. "We kinda jumped right over the trying part."

His brain simply ceased firing, and he could only stare. "You're... We're... How?"

"Remember that night we got engaged out in the orchard? We sort of skipped a step."

His mind helpfully replayed the sight of her, naked and gorgeous, sinking down onto him without a single thought to a condom. He went hard in an instant as his body made a bid for a repeat. But that wasn't why she was here, looking at him with big, worried eyes.

"We're having a baby? For Christmas?"

"It seems we are."

Kyle thought he might burst with joy. "Best Christmas present ever!"

One golden brow winged up. "Not a wedding present?"

"You're my wedding present. There's nothing better than that." He pulled her close, intending to kiss her, but stopped. "I have a feeling if I muss you up, someone's going to have my head."

Her mouth curved in a saucy grin. "Then I guess we need to finish this wedding business so we can get to the mussing portion of the program."

At the heated look in her eyes, he stepped back. "Get on out of here before I give in to temptation."

"I do hope you will give in to all the temptations. Later." She backed toward the door and blew him a kiss. "See you at the end of the aisle."

As soon as she slipped out, he sank down onto the bed and exhaled a slow breath.

A baby. He was gonna be a father. Holy shit.

Running both hands through his hair, he waited for the news to really sink in. But it was too big, too good to fully absorb.

The door opened again, and Caleb stepped in. "It's time."

Kyle stood, firming up knees that felt a little like Jell-O. "Let's do this."

Caleb eyed him. "You okay, man?"

Kyle clapped a hand on his shoulder. "Brother, I am fucking perfect. Absolutely nothing could make this day any better."

But as he stood at the head of the long aisle that ran through the east orchard, beneath the fragrant blooming apple trees, and watched the woman he loved walk toward him in the dress he'd bought her, to a song he'd written her, on her grandfather's arm, he spotted the plastic ring on a chain around her throat and knew he'd been wrong. That was the absolute cherry on top. And as they finally executed that long-ago marriage pact and faced their guests as man and wife, he knew their adventure was just beginning.

CHOOSE YOUR NEXT ROMANCE

NEXT UP IN the Men of the Misfit Inn series is Wyatt Sullivan. If you're a fan of *Fixer Upper* or HGTV in general, you're gonna *love this book.*

After a lifetime spent trying to prove he's not a screw up, contractor Wyatt Sullivan is ready to take his YouTube channel, *DIWyatt,* to the big time. But he needs more than the one-man flips that built his reputation. He needs something truly big to impress network execs enough to give him his own home improvement show.

After a messy, ugly divorce, publicist Deanna James can't afford another mistake. So when she wakes up from a night of too much wine to find out she's bought a historic monstrosity of a house in an online auction, she panics. If she's going to sell it and not lose her shirt to her ex-husband, she's going to need some serious help. But how will she afford it?

Wyatt's just the guy to ride to her rescue. He'll take on the job if she'll let him film the process. Deanna sweetens the deal with the added bonus of using her PR skills to raise the profile of *DIWyatt* enough to impress the suits. There's just one problem: They both have to move in.

As they battle home improvement hell and rising attraction, can they keep from giving the viewers more of a show than they ever intended?

Grab your copy of *Don't You Wanna Stay* today!

Meanwhile, have you explored the *Rescue My Heart* series? This trilogy follows three former Army Rangers navigating their post-military lives and finding love long the way. It's set in Eden's Ridge, so there are plenty of cameos from our Misfit Inn favorites, as well as Kyle's publicist Deanna, who's a friend of Ivy Blake in *Baby It's Cold Outside*.

OTHER BOOKS BY KAIT NOLAN

A complete and up-to-date list of all my books can be found at https://kaitnolan.com.

THE MISFIT INN SERIES
SMALL TOWN FAMILY ROMANCE

- *When You Got A Good Thing* (Kennedy and Xander)

- *Til There Was You* (Misty and Denver)
- *Those Sweet Words* (Pru and Flynn)
- *Stay A Little Longer* (Athena and Logan)
- *Bring It On Home* (Maggie and Porter)

RESCUE MY HEART SERIES
SMALL TOWN MILITARY ROMANCE

- *Baby It's Cold Outside* (Ivy and Harrison)
- *What I Like About You* (Laurel and Sebastian)
- *Bad Case of Loving You* (Paisley and Ty prequel)
- *Made For Loving You* (Paisley and Ty)

MEN OF THE MISFIT INN
SMALL TOWN SOUTHERN ROMANCE

- *Let It Be Me* (Emerson and Caleb)

- *Our Kind of Love* (Abbey and Kyle)
- *Don't You Wanna Stay* (Deanna and Wyatt)

WISHFUL SERIES
SMALL TOWN SOUTHERN ROMANCE

- *Once Upon A Coffee* (Avery and Dillon)
- *To Get Me To You* (Cam and Norah)
- *Know Me Well* (Liam and Riley)
- *Be Careful, It's My Heart* (Brody and Tyler)
- *Just For This Moment* (Myles and Piper)
- *Wish I Might* (Reed and Cecily)
- *Turn My World Around* (Tucker and Corinne)
- *Dance Me A Dream* (Jace and Tara)
- *See You Again* (Trey and Sandy)
- *The Christmas Fountain* (Chad and Mary Alice)

- *You Were Meant For Me* (Mitch and Tess)
- *A Lot Like Christmas* (Ryan and Hannah)
- *Dancing Away With My Heart* (Zach and Lexi)

WISHING FOR A HERO SERIES (A WISHFUL SPINOFF SERIES)
SMALL TOWN ROMANTIC SUSPENSE

- *Make You Feel My Love* (Judd and Autumn)
- *Watch Over Me* (Nash and Rowan)
- *Can't Take My Eyes Off You* (Ethan and Miranda)
- *Burn For You* (Sean and Delaney)

MEET CUTE ROMANCE
SMALL TOWN SHORT ROMANCE

- *Once Upon A Snow Day*
- *Once Upon A New Year's Eve*

- *Once Upon An Heirloom*
- *Once Upon A Coffee*
- *Once Upon A Campfire*
- *Once Upon A Rescue*

SUMMER CAMP
CONTEMPORARY ROMANCE

- *Once Upon A Campfire*
- *Second Chance Summer*

ABOUT KAIT

Kait is a Mississippi native, who often swears like a sailor, calls everyone sugar, honey, or darlin', and can wield a bless your heart like a saber or a Snuggie, depending on requirements.

You can find more information on this RITA ® Award-winning author and her books on her website http://kaitnolan.com.

Do you need more small town sass and spark? Sign up for her newsletter to hear about new releases, book deals, and exclusive content!

www.ingramcontent.com/pod-product-compliance
Lightning Source LLC
Chambersburg PA
CBHW060224100726
47907CB00003B/490